TIM KERN

Like Murder Like Son

MYSTERY ONE™ SERIES

LIKE MURDER LIKE SON

LIKE MURDER
LIKE SON

FIRST EDITION

Like Murder   Like Son

Tim Kern

<u>Acknowledgments</u>

Many thanks are extended to the readers of my earlier books, who encouraged me to keep writing, always in hope that the next book would be better.

To fellow novelists Claudia Pfeiffer and Chuck Holmes, whose insights and ideas enriched the story, kept it between the lines, and honed the characters.

To Detective Mark Brizendine of the Anderson, Indiana PD, whose idea for the murder weapon got me to rewrite major parts of the book, and whose insight into general police procedures kept it believable.

Special thanks to Peggy Vore, who helped me with location work in Columbus, Ohio.

To lenneluce of Fiverr, for the cover drawing.

To my good friend Drew, who suggested that my first book's murder was too mild and my second book's multiple murders bordered on being too grisly, I hope you find that this book's killings are *just right*.

…and thank you to my life's inspiration, Robyne.

-ooo-

LIKE MURDER   LIKE SON

LIKE MURDER   LIKE SON

TIM KERN

Contents

Chapter One: The roommates

A year earlier, nearly to the day, Ted and Lew were first contemplating "living on their own" in Columbus. Freshman orientation at OSU would start tomorrow, and the two had just found out they were to be roommates. Lewis Foreman was a year older than Ted, a six-foot mixed-race son of an abusive dad who had been a guard at the Chillicothe Correctional Institution. Lew planned on carrying a pre-med major with a psychology minor.

Ted Hamlin signed on as a chemistry major. Built light and quick, he liked soccer and cross-country, '60s and '70s rock, and, like Lew, girls.

But Lew was much more experienced in that department. "I mean," he was saying on their first day walking around campus together, "You're really a virgin, for real?"

"Yeah. A lot of my friends are. What's the big deal?"

"How long you plan to save yourself?"

"Well, that's not exactly why I came to school. I'm here to learn chemistry, maybe play some soccer."

"You didn't give me an answer, Ted."

"Can we talk about that later?"

"Sure. We've got forever. But would you mind helping me out?"

"What can I do? You've got all the experience, remember?"

"I need a wing man, somebody to scout around, find the kind of girls I'm gonna want to meet, help peel them away from their packs…"

"How am I going to know what you like?"

"Look, Ted. Do you know what a 'killer body' is?"

"The original Britney Spears? Beyoncé?" Ted noddedm Lewis continued. "You watch *Star Trek?* Seven of Nine?"

"Not a trekker."

"Anything from Hani – you know Hani? – to Jennifer Lawrence to JayLo. You watch old movies? Sofia Loren, Ann-Margret, Grace Kelly."

"I don't know those last ones."

"Doesn't matter," Lewis said. "We're just practicing today, anyway. When you see one that's at least an eight, you'll say where to look. Like, if she's a nine, straight in front of us, you'll say, 'nine, at twelve o'clock.' Twelve is straight ahead, like the hands on a clock. So, where is three o'clock?"

"Ninety degrees to our left."

"To our right. But yeah, you get it. Let's do a little practice, just to get our rating system in synch. See that girl over there, just crossing the street? You see her, you say, 'eight, at one o'-clock,' because she's a little to our right, and she's, well, nearly an eight. Seven, probably, but you get the idea, right?"

"Looks like an eight to me," Ted said.

"That's 'cuz you're horny and maybe you don't have high enough standards. There are some fine girls here. Don't sell yourself short. Maintain your objectivity. Tell her she's the most beautiful thing you've ever seen when it'll get you some. Here, look. There's a six, right over there, two o'clock. What would you have called her?"

"Probably a seven, eight maybe. In Mansfield, anyway."

"She's a six here. Don't bother me with the marginal ones. Well, okay, if you see something unusual or special, like way long hair or super-sexy clothes, or if she's driving a Ferrari."

"Yeah, right. Okay." Ted looked around. "Okay, eight at six o'clock. Agree?"

Lewis turned around and took inventory. "Yeah, she has a super-sexy walk, nice ass. Did you see her face?"

"I thought we were just doing bodies."

"Yeah, that's fine for now. We'll get better at this when we've been doing it a while. Good call. Well, let's head back to the dorm and make sure we know where all the stuff is – laundry room… whatever."

They walked, Ted spotting, Lewis giving feedback as they went. Then Lew threw him a new term. "There's a nine straight ahead. She's a MILF, but she's a nine. Oh, wait, an eight. Anyway, what do you think?"

"I think you're nuts. That's somebody's mother. What's a MILF?"

"Oh, man, don't you know *any*thing in Mansfield? Of course she's somebody's mother. MILF means 'a mom I'd love to'…"

"Okay, I get it. That's… that's disgusting."

"Says you. Did you ever have an older woman? You know, late thirties, forty? Forty-five? …Oh, that's right. You're a virgin."

"Yeah, and if you're going to hook me up with old ladies, I'm going to stay one for a long time."

"Ted, you just don't know, do you? The very best lovin' on the planet is with women who know what they're doing. That's wasted on a virgin, so don't worry about it until next semester at least. Don't get me wrong, though. Girls our age can be hot, and if you get the right reputation, they're easy, too."

"Don't worry," Ted said. "Yuck. *Moms*?" He perked up. "Eight, at two o'clock. How 'm I doing?"

"That's a good call, bro. Keep 'em coming." They kept walking, nearly at their dorm now, and Lewis lit up, poking Ted with his elbow. "Dead ahead, er… twelve o'clock. Holy sh… Man, you see that MILF? Now, I don't care how old she is. Even at this distance, that's a solid ten. Nice brown hair. Mmmm… my favorite. Look at those legs, that tan."

The object of Lew's attention stopped walking, looked around, as if she were trying to get her bearings. Her crisp white blouse, rather than looking businessslike, just helped emphasize her supple brown leather skirt, tight but not straining, shining in the sunlight on sleek hips. "Oh, god, that butt. Great tits, too. Purrr-fection. And she walks like…Ted, you looking? Ted? *Ted*, what's the matter with you? You've got to appreciate that. That's pure *art*, man. I bet she's…"

Ted stopped walking and Lewis turned around to face him. "What's wrong, roomie?"

"That's my mom."

Chapter Two: Settling in

"Hi, Ted," she said, and she gave him a hug. "Who's your friend?"

"Oh, Mom, this is Lewis, my roommate. He's in pre-med. He's from Chillicothe."

"Lewis Foreman. Pleased to meet you, Missus Hamlin."

"Hello, Lewis. You can just call me Jill." Then to Ted, "May I see your room?"

"Mom, we're… Do you really want to see it? It's a mess. We just started unpacking."

She turned. "Lewis, do you mind?"

"Ummm, well, okay, but like Ted said, it's a mess." He tried to speak normally. Difficult, since Ted was standing on his shoe, pressing down hard.

The elevator ride to the third floor was quiet. Four other freshman boys were there. Two of them were checking out Ted's mom, as she stood at the front, waiting for the door to open. Ted turned red.

Door opened and Ted said, "Here we are, Mom, three twenty-seven. It's to the right." And she let him go in front, fishing for his key. Lewis lagged behind, far enough back to enjoy the view.

"Well, you're right," she said. "It is a mess."

The bunked beds were on the left side, two desks along the 'dormitory-green' wall to the right. You could walk through the middle to the far wall, which had a wheezy air conditioner/heater below the full-width window. The north exposure revealed more dorms, some grass, sidewalks, hundreds of new students, some carrying boxes or dragging two-wheel dollies or walking their bicycles through the dense pedestrian traffic, because everyone jammed up the sidewalks, afraid to breach the edges of the concrete. The closets were at the door end of the room, one on the side by the desks, the other at the end of the bunk beds. Jill looked around, as if there were anything she couldn't see immediately.

"It's… nice," she said. "Or at least it could be, once you get your stuff put away, maybe hang some things on the walls. Could I ask, are all the rooms like this?"

Lewis answered. "On the odd-numbered floors, they're green, like this. They're tan…"

"Beige," Ted interrupted.

"Beige on the even-numbered floors. Everybody on this side of the building has the same view, more or less. The other side, they see the river. Most of the freshmen are in 'quads,' you know, four to a room. But there's a few smaller rooms with just two. That's us."

"I meant, the furniture arrangement. Is everybody in bunk beds?"

"We thought we'd have more floor space," Ted said, "if we stacked 'em up. And see," he made a grand sweep of a couple uncovered floor tiles, "we do. We're going to put shelves there. Maybe bricksand wood, or those plastic milk crates. They stack."

Jill swallowed. "I'll vote for the milk crates. Deeper, less likely to fall over on you." Then she looked at her watch – almost four – and said, "Well, you boys are here for the long haul, and I have an hour back to Mansfield. Have fun, study hard, and don't forget to write. Or email, or text, or something. Call. Oh, hell – stay in touch." And she kissed Ted on the forehead and left through the still-open door.

"I'll walk you to your car," Lewis called, and was out before Ted could stop him.

* * *

"Missus…"

"Jill. Just call me Jill."

"Missus… er, Jill, I just want to make sure you get through campus okay."

"You're from Chillicothe? You seem to have good manners. That's good. I've tried to raise Ted that way, too. Watch out for each other, okay?"

Lewis nodded, started to turn away. Jill grabbed his arm, kept talking. "Don't get into trouble. First semester, that's a big adjustment. That's when most of the 'party crowd' flunks out. Second semester is a lot more serious, when they're gone."

"Oh, I'll be careful, thank you, Missus… Jill. And I think Ted and I will get along great. Yes, Chillicothe. My dad was a guard at the prison, the

Chillicothe Correctional Institution. He died three years ago."

"I'm sorry, Lewis," she said. "Losing a father is tough on a boy that age." Then, "Ted's father passed away, too. He was killed in a car accident when Ted was just two. Blizzard, while he was driving home from work in Findlay. Ted didn't get to know him, he was so little." Then she brightened up. "But Ted has always dreamed of going to Ohio State, and here he is. Chemistry? I don't know why he picked that. He did well in it in high school, but this is the big league."

"Big league," Lew repeated.

"Oh, I'm right here, Lewis. Thank you for the walk. And remember – you and Ted be serious about studying."

"We will, …uhhh, Jill. Don't worry. We will." He walked back to Room 327, never looking back and without touching the ground.

* * *

"I don't care if you are my roommate," said Ted. "You say one thing about my mother, you even look at her, and I'll…"

"Chill, bro. I just walked her to her car. Left her right there, by the black Buick SUV."

Ted smiled. *She doesn't have a black Buick SUV. She has a dark green Taurus. Smart Mom.* "Well, okay. You understand why I'm protective, especially after your MILF lecture and all. Just remember, she's my mom."

"Yeah, yeah, okay. Sorry 'bout that. I didn't know. Let's get this shit put away."

"Yeah, fine. I got top bunk."

"I wanted the bottom anyway," Lewis said, "And I get the desk by the door."

"Cool. I wanted the one by the window, anyway." They both laughed. "And I already took this closet," he said, nodding to the closet on the bed side.

"I don't care. You can't open it when the hall door's open."

"Crap," Ted said, as Lewis laughed.

* * *

Saturday night, and Ted and Lewis didn't want to sit around the dorm. "Got any money?" Ted asked.

"Not for going out. Hey, let's look around campus, see if there's other kids' going places, maybe a party, or see where we can walk to."

Walking without purpose, traveling with the crowd, Ted and Lew practiced their bird-dogging and got their rating system in synch. "Why d'you only want eights and nines, Lew? Why not a six or seven, or a ten?"

"A ten is a waste of time. Too much competition, and they're always ready to go with a new guy, one with more money. Seniors or grad students, guys with jobs, living off-campus. Forget tens."

"What's wrong with sixes and sevens?"

"Why bother with a six, when you can get an eight?"

"Because… there's more than looks? Because she's nice? Because she's smart, or interested in you? Because you've got a lot in common? I mean, hell, a six is still above average, you know."

"Why not a one, then?"

"Standards, Lew. You gotta have standards. If you're a one, then fine, Go get a one."

"What makes you think you're *not* a one?"

Ted took up a mock boxing stance, punched the air in front of his roommate's face. "You're such a shit." They both laughed.

They edged into the crowd at the doorway of one of the sit-down burger joints all crowded with students. Nowhere to sit, barely a place to stand. Friends from last year were finding each other, catching up on what happened over the summer and on long-gone graduates. Class schedules, GPAs, professors, summer jobs. Boyfriends, girlfriends, and a few weddings.

Ted and Lewis were new. Nobody knew them. They didn't have anything to catch up about. As freshmen, they were anonymous, if not invisible. Ted kicked Lewis's shoe. "Eights at three o'-clock."

Lewis casually turned his body to the right and saw the three girls. *Probably frosh. Nobody's talking to them, either.*

He said, "Which one you like? Not the red-head."

"What's wrong with the redhead?"

"Nothing at all that I can see. You want the blonde? She's hot, or she could be."

"No," said Ted. "The darker blonde. She looks nice. She's the quiet one, anyway."

"Okay, let's roll. Follow my lead, grasshopper."

"Grasshopper?"

"Just… let's go."

* * *

Rebecca, the hot blonde, sensed them coming, and turned her back to them. Lewis came around the right, where the redhead was trying to look like she was not paying attention.

"Hi. I'm Lewis."

"Nicole." She turned away from her friends, shooting a glance at the blonde, who now faced Jessica, the darker-haired girl.

But Ted was already distracting her. "I'm Ted," he said. "Are you waiting for a table?"

"Jessica. No, we're just talking. I'm a freshman. This is Rachel," she nodded at the blonde, who barely nodded back, "and my friend from Waterloo, Nicole," and the redhead turned away from Ted after saying a quick and bored, "Hi."

"What's your major, Jessica?"

"Chemistry. Physics minor. You?"

"Chem, too. I don't have a minor picked out yet. Do you have all your classes?"

Jessica said, "I got my important ones. I'm going to register for the junk classes tomorrow. Didn't have time today. Stood in line too long, to get the chemistry one-ten and physics I wanted.

"I got my chemistry today, too. Monday, Tuesday, Thursday at eight. That's the one I wanted. Get it over with early."

She smiled. "Me, too," she said. "Gronka?" Ted nodded, remembering the strange name. "Sounds like a professor, doesn't he? Gronka. What else are your registering for?"

Lewis was posing for Nicole, and she, long and thin but with oversized tits that she was quite aware of in a tight white t-shirt, was subconsciously moving to the first stanza of what looked like a mating dance. "What are you taking? What's your major?"

Nicole answered, "Psychology. I think people are interesting. I'm a people-watcher, a people person. And dogs and horses, but that's not psych, really."

"I like animals, too," Lewis said, "people – not so much." And they laughed. "You taking any evening classes?"

"Just Tuesday, six 'til nine. Some required English course."

"So you're free after nine on Tuesdays?"

Nicole started to turn slowly away, lightly touching his elbow. "Some Tuesdays," shooting him a smile over her shoulder as she hooked up with Rachel again and they walked to the bathroom.

Jessica and Ted had gotten a tiny round stand-up table and were nursing a couple root beer floats. Lewis walked over and smiled at the petite chemistry major.

"Hi, I'm Lewis. You know this guy?" as he nodded toward Ted. Ted didn't look like he wanted to be interrupted just then, so Lew continued. "We just met, and already we're sleeping together."

Ted straightened up. "Get the hell outta here, Lewis," and the taller one left. Jessica's mouth was open.

"We're just roommates," Ted said. "I didn't know him before today, but maybe I'll have to kill him some day."

Jessica laughed, her eyes lighting up. "Sorry, Ted, but that was funny. Not what he did – that was mean, considering he didn't know how I'd take it – but your *face*. That was priceless." She laughed again.

Ted started to blush, either out of anger or embarrassment, he wasn't sure which, and he didn't care. But Jessica continued. "You looked so surprised. Of course I knew you two weren't gay. And you look so handsome when you're about to explode with rage." She leaned toward him, put her finger on his nose, and gave a tiny push.

"Your friend, the redhead," Ted said, "I think he likes her."

"Everybody does, at first," she said. "Some more than others. Some longer. We went to high school together. She's a man-eater."

"Should I tell him?"

"What, and spoil it? No. Hey, who knows? They may be perfect for each other. At least, if he can ever get her phone number."

"She's long gone tonight," Ted said.

"So, do you want *my* phone number?"

Chapter Three: Jack

"Jill, that was fantastic. What was that all about?" He rolled back to his side of the bed, totally spent, the last of daylight fading outside the hotel window.

"You're a sweet man. Not just in the typical way. You think of nice things to do. Thanks for letting me use your car while you were sitting in that dingy waiting room, reading two-year-old *Motor Trends* as I was saying good-bye to Ted. He's so grown up. I miss him. He's never been away from home more than a week.

"Other men, they think an occasional bunch of roses or some trinket matters. You understand."

"Jill, baby. I'd like to give you diamonds and pearls, but your poor old Taurus – it needed tires something awful, and winter's just around the corner. And you didn't even know your brakes were shot. It's not romantic, but it's my way of taking care of you. I had no idea you'd like them so much," as he got out of bed and went out to the kitchen to pour two bourbons, hers with a couple ice cubes. He edged the bedroom door open with his bare foot. "And you like bourbon. You're all right, Jill Hamlin."

Jack Pope was fifty-something, a perennially-recovering alcoholic lawyer from Dayton, two hours away. A couple generations before he was born, a brilliant crook started NCR, the cash register company, making a fortune by building great cash registers (and deliberately-faulty exact copies – right down to the nameplate -- of the competitor's cheaper machines). That brilliant crook's fortune started Jack on a path to good schools, then law school. It put him in Dayton's elite society, along with the Wrights and others who made Dayton a hot town a hundred-plus years earlier. And it kept him there, even as his own law practice, aided by the connections to all the right people and organizations, made him an attractive prospect for a future divorce, which came to fruition, making him available to Jill, who didn't care about 'society,' but who liked this fat old well-dressed man's attention. *For a big guy, he's easy to maneuver,* she thought.

"And you, too, Jack Pope. 'Jack Pope.' Sounds like a cop in a TV series. You know, 'Jack Pope, his small but obviously strong belt buckle preceding him by several inches to the stand, where he swore to tell the truth, the whole truth,...'" She laughed.

"Hey, wait a minute. You know I've lost forty pounds since we started going out. I'm really working on it."

"Sorry, Jack. I just let my mind run free there. You have been making progress, and I hope it's for you, not for me. You needed to lose that weight. But I was talking about 'Jack Pope.' It just sounds like a cop, that's all."

"It's kind of silly, I guess. I was called John for most of my young life. Then in 1978, Pope Paul the Sixth died, and the new pope called himself John Paul the First. My parents were super-Catholics. Anyway, he died,..."

"Who? The new pope?"

"Yeah, he died in, like a month or two, and the next pope – he's officially a saint now – he called himself Pope John Paul the Second."

"So?"

"So – and here's where being hyper-Catholic comes in – so, my parents thought that my name, John Paul Pope, was now sacrilegious, especially on, you know, the first day of school, when they call your name backwards by the alphabet. 'Pope, John Paul' brought the house down. So they started making everybody call me Jack. My oldest friends still call me John."

"Which do you prefer that I call you?"

"I'd say 'Jack' is just fine. But if you like John, go ahead. I can handle it."

"Well, er... Jack, were you named after anybody in particular? Family tradition, all that?"

"No, I was actually named after John Paul Jones, the Revolutionary War hero. You know, the guy who shouted, 'I have not yet begun to fight!' when his ship was getting sunk."

"Sorta remember that. He didn't sink, did he?"

"Well, yeah, his ship sank. But he won the battle and captured the British ship than sank him. So why are we talking about this?"

"I don't know. It started with 'Jack Pope,' the cop's name."

"Okay, why are you called Jill?"

"It seems my mom always wanted to be named Jill, and she wasn't, so she named me Jill."

"What was her name?"

"Mildred."

"Oh, god."

"So, would you like another drink?"

"No, but how about another dose of Jack Pope?"

"Babe, you've already worn me out. Don't get me wrong. It was worth it, and I can't wait to do that again."

"Me neither. Well, come snuggle up to me, old man. Tomorrow is another day, and we've both got to go home in the morning."

Chapter Four: Thanksgiving at Ted's

The leaves had turned. Brilliant colors covered campus, growing thicker on the ground and thinner on the trees. "Mom," Ted said, hanging his backpack off one shoulder and holding his cell phone with the other hand, trying to get back to the dorm, a little harried and irritated. "We're like, just an hour away... The leaves are great here, too. Not that I had any time to see them until after mid-terms… I did okay, I think. These general ed courses are so stupid and boring. All this freshman-year stuff. Just junk fill, nothing to do with chemistry. I understand the math courses, basic writing, even. But why do I have to take fine arts?"

"It's to make you a well-rounded adult."

"It's to give tenured old professors someone to talk to, is what it's for. Nobody'd take these useless courses if we didn't have to. If I ever want to study underwater basket weaving, I'll take a course at the Y."

"Anyway, how's chemistry?"

"It's chem one-ten. It's more of a review, not really anything new. They say it gets hard next semester, so we've all got to be sure we're ready. It doesn't hurt, but it's pretty boring."

"Then you'll get an A in it?"

"Yeah, but don't count on an A in Modern European History."

"You're taking *that?*"

"Yeah, one of those general ed things. Looked less-stupid than Middle English Poetry. It's maybe interesting a little, but it takes more time away from the stuff that matters to my major. We're finally getting into the good stuff – the rise and fall of communism, that kind of thing, so it's cool."

"Well, I'm glad you're working on it, Ted. What I called about, how many days do you get for Thanksgiving? I haven't seen you since I dropped you off."

"Well, as you know, it's busy here. But yeah, I'd like to come home for a few days. We get five days. They're shutting down Tuesday night, but everybody's cutting Tuesday, for sure the afternoon courses, so I'll be done by eleven. What time were you thinking of being here?"

"I can come at eleven-thirty. We'll be home by two or so, eat along the way."

"That would be great, Mom, but you know I'll have to study a little at home. There's still work to do, even though it's a holiday."

Ted opened the dorm room, looked at Lewis, who was half-asleep on the lower bunk, and tossed his backpack into his chair as his mom said, "I won't get in your way. It'll just be nice to see you."

"I love you, Mom. Thanks."

"Oh – and Ted?"

"Yeah?"

"Your roommate, Lewis, is he going home for Thanksgiving, or what?"

"I don't know. I didn't ask him."

"Maybe he'd like to come have Thanksgiving dinner with us. Is he there? Can you put him on?

"Mom, I…"

"Is he there?"

"…Hi, Missus, er… Jill." Ted shot him a look, restrained yet threatening.

"Hello, Lewis. Ted and I were wondering if you'd like to join us for Thanksgiving. Of course, if you have other plans…"

"Well, I, ummm, I don't know. I haven't talked with my mom yet."

"Well, you let Ted know. You're welcome in Mansfield. We have a nice guest room and wifi."

"Thank you, uhhh, Jill. I'll be sure to let Ted know, as soon as I talk to my mom. Here's Ted."

Ted took the phone. "Mom, that's nice of you and all, but, well, Lew's got a family, too, and…"

"Just let me know."

"Okay, Mom. I will. I love you…. 'Bye." Phone off. He glared at Lewis.

"Dude, I didn't… I didn't do anything. She asked *me*." He took a breath, calmed down, changed direction. "Besides, of all the places I've never been, Mansfield's one of them. Do they still do tours at that spooky prison? That'd be cool."

"Yeah, they do, I think. My dad worked there before it closed. It closed, like ten years before I was born."

"Your mom said he died in a blizzard, coming home from… somewhere."

"Findlay. He was working at their jail. After Mansfield closed, he worked a lot of places, I guess. I was like, two when he died. I don't remember him, just what Mom and the relatives tell me, and some pictures."

"My dad died three years ago. Weird, he was a prison guard, too. In Chillicothe."

"Sorry, man."

"Don't be. He was an asshole most of the time. He's where I get my temper, but I don't want to be like him. He beat me, hit Sherry…"

"That sucks. So, Sherry's your stepmom?"

"Yeah, it sucks. Yeah, stepmom. My real mom died when I was an infant." Lewis got back on track. "Like I say, I don't want to be like him. He drank too much. Kept us poor. He was always wrecking cars. Mean…"

"How did he die?"

"Somebody killed him. Shot him, right in front of our house when he came home from work. Never solved, but it was probably one of the guys got let out."

"One of the prisoners? You know which one?"

"Like I said, he was mean to us, probably to everybody there, too. Could have been anybody, pretty much."

"They didn't figure out…?"

"I don't think they liked him, either. Sherry and I don't think they tried very hard to catch the guy who shot him."

"Sorry, man."

"Yeah, well…"

"You ready for food?"

"How now, ground cow?" They laughed.

* * *

After meatloaf, mashed potatoes, and spaghetti, Ted was full, but he couldn't hold back the wondering. "Lew, you said your dad was murdered, right there in front of your house, but they never caught the guy who did it."

"They seemed to feel bad for Sherry. Anyway, they were nice to Sherry, but they didn't seem all that interested in who did it. They took pictures, did an autopsy – who needs an autopsy when there's three bullet holes in the guy's heart and another one in the back of his head? – and the usual stuff, but they didn't even ask around the neighborhood, or anything."

"So that's why you call her 'Sherry' instead of 'mom.' Weren't you an infant?"

"No. Dad and I were alone for maybe a year. I don't remember, and I never really cared. Anyway, they were together a few years, then they finally got married when I was eleven. Dad didn't want to confuse me, I guess. She was uncomfortable with 'mom,' she said. So I've always called her Sherry. Besides, you know how many questions I'd get" – he pointed to his face – "with my 'mom' a freckled redhead?"

"Yeah," Ted laughed. "What are you, anyway?" He tried to not have said that. "What's your ethnic background, I mean?"

"Heh. I'm officially a mutt. All-American, from Jamaica, Samoa, India, Persia. And I'm Basque and Urdu, too, they say. But they don't know. I mean, it's probably impossible to get all the ingredients together for that recipe. So I'm 'mixed.' I'm a Mongrel-American. But there's not a lot of redhead and freckles in here."

Ted was smiling.

"What?"

"That's pretty impossible, all right. Urdu is a language, not a nationality."

"So screw you, white boy." And they were both laughing, now.

"You ever try one of those DNA tests?"
"No. Why – you think they'll find out I'm Irish?"

* * *

The ride to Mansfield was quiet. The old Taurus was noisy, but Jill kept it on the road as Ted and Lewis studied, getting ahead on their reading. "Are you boys hungry?" she said, town approaching.

Ted said, "Now that you mention it, you know what I miss most, while I'm eating dorm food all the time?" Jill waited for 'a home-cooked meal,' but he said, "a Big Mac."

Lewis joined in. "Two all beef patties, special sauce,..."

"Just quit it, boys!" She faked offense. "Okay, Mickey-D's it is," and she pulled in. "Let's get out of the car for a few minutes."

* * *

The Taurus groaned its way up the steep driveway and into the tidy one-car garage.

"Here, Lew. Here's the guest room. Follow me." Ted pointed down the hall. "That's my mom's room on the left. Mine's on the right, here. Then your room. Bathroom's across from your room, end of the hall."

"Thanks, man." And he went to the guest room at the end of the hall.

It was small, ten by twelve feet, with a window looking out on the back yard, overgrown a little, especially over by the chainlink fence that separated it from an empty field. White walls, a blue checked bedspread on the twin bed, a matching pillow sham over a tired pillow. There were a table, chair, dresser, and a closet that was already full of boxes of... something, and a shelf that had hats on it. Cowboy boots, small ones but fancy, and some shoes were on the floor.

Lewis put his backpack on the bed and emptied its contents into one of the dresser drawers, took his toothbrush, deodorant, and razor and put them on the table, pushed them to the edge. He put his books next to his other stuff, unpacked his laptop, and plugged it in, then plugged his phone into it.

Knock on the door, and Jill entered.

"Hello, Missus, er... Jill."

"Hi," she said, and walked to the window, looked out at the November-brown desolation.

"Look, ...Jill," he said.

She turned to face him.

"Look, I'm just not comfortable calling you Jill."

"What would you like to call me, Lewis?"

"Uhhh, Missus Hamlin okay?"

"Makes me feel old. How about Miss Jill? Would that work for you?"

"Okay. It's better, anyway. I'll try it. Thanks."

She said, "Good. Try it," and she brushed past him, making obvious contact as she slipped into the hallway.

* * *

"Mom, can I drive Lew around town, show him stuff?"

"Ted, it's Thanksgiving. Everything will be closed."

"We won't be gone long." He laughed. "There's not that much to see."

"Be back by seven. Love you, Ted."

"Love you, too, Mom."

They piled into the old Taurus. "Do we have time to see the prison?" Lewis said. "We can see it from the outside before it gets dark, I guess. You'll recognize some of it from the movies. They did a couple movies there. *Air Force One, Fallen Angels...*"

"And *Shawshank Redemption.*"

"Yeah, you're right. That's the biggest one. And a couple more, probably. It's right up here. We can't get in, but nobody will stop us walking around a little."

They didn't park in the lot. Pulled over on the shoulder. It was closer, anyway. The sun was going down, so they walked fast, then stumbled into a run. Lewis pulled out his cell phone and took a few pictures, as Ted pointed out some of the most memorable viewpoints. "That gate," he said, "is almost always one of the shots. And the wing over there..."

"What's that sign?" Lewis couldn't read it.

"It says 'no pictures,' because that, over there, that's the new prison and they don't want you taking pictures of it. You might be plotting a breakout."

"Yeah, like it's not on Google Earth or something."

"Don't do it, Lew. It's stupid, but they're real serious about it."

"Hell, Ted, I don't give a rat's ass. Don't worry. Let's go around to the other side before it gets too dark."

A Sheriff's car swept around the building and pulled up to the boys. "You're going to have to leave here," the deputy sheriff said through his open window. "It's Thanksgiving; they're closed, and you're trespassing. Go home, boys. Is that your car up there?"

"Yes, sir," Ted said. "We'll get out of here. Yes, that's my car. Have a happy Thanksgiving, officer."

"You, too. But don't come back again until they're open, okay?" He waited until they got in the car before he moved. As they left, he followed them out to the main road. They turned right; he went left.

* * *

It was dark when they got to Ted's place. "Do they teach you boys to tell time in college?" Jill had expected them to be late, and had planned dinner for eight. It was seven-twenty. "Go get cleaned up."

"Mom, we went to the old prison, and..."

"Get cleaned up. *Go!* Show me your pictures after dinner."

"Miss Jill, I'm sorry we're late. It was my fault. I wanted to hang out a little longer, and then the police came and…"

"The po*lice?* Lewis..."

"Oh, he was real nice and all. Just wanted us gone. No trouble."

"Well, there's going to be trouble if you're not gone from here in about three seconds. Dinner's waiting. *Scat!*" And she smacked him on the butt as he headed past her.

Dinner was classic, with sweet potatoes on the side, mashed potatoes and dark gravy, and a small turkey from Boston Market. "Perfect as always, Mom," Ted said.

"Really good, Miss Jill. Definitely not dorm food."

"I'll clean up," she said, "and you can relax, study, whatever. We have a ton of channels. The remote's on the table by the sofa."

Ted and Lewis retired to their rooms. Lew soon reappeared briefly, turning the corner to the bathroom, towel, brush, and razor in hand. He was back in his room minutes later.

Jill put the leftovers in the fridge, set the dishwasher to working, took a quick shower, put on her bathrobe, turned on the TV, and collapsed on the couch. Ted tried to read a textbook for a few minutes, but nothing was registering, so he took his shower and then soon fell asleep.

* * *

Lewis couldn't sleep. It wasn't the low mumblings from the television. It wasn't the third helping of sweet potatoes with brown sugar and cinnamon. It was Jill. Something, he didn't know what. He got that glance from her as he left the dinner table, that strange glance he had never noticed from an older woman, but that he had spotted at parties, that glance that took just a little too long, that went from his eyes to below his belt, and then to his mouth, before returning to his eyes, as though she had been looking at his eyes the whole time.

And she's, damn, she's Ted's mom. But she is just so... hot. He tried to sleep, but he couldn't. The TV was still on. *Maybe we should talk.*

Lewis got out of bed, pulled on his pajamas, and walked quietly to the living room. Jill was sitting on the couch, slouched all the way back, her feet on the coffee table, *maybe asleep*. He sat down next to her, and she opened her eyes for a moment but said nothing.

She leaned into him, cuddling. He put his arm around her shoulder, and she snuggled closer, and dropped her hand between his knees, just there, maybe a bit higher, with a little pressure.

Lewis tried to relax, but part of him couldn't, being hard as a rock and all.

She's just trying to sleep. She doesn't mean anything. Forcing the lie on himself wasn't working. Still, he tried. *She really doesn't mean it. She...*

She moved her hand up, as far as it could go, but didn't move, just let out a little sigh, as if she were snuggling in for the night. Lewis was about to explode, and she opened her eyes and looked at him. She moved both her hands behind his head, cradling it and pulling it closer to her face, until their eyes could no longer focus. So they closed them. And they kissed.

She stood up and took his hand, walked him to his bedroom, and yanked him down on her, on the floor. Her robe fell away. Only her arms were covered. "The bed squeaks," she whispered. He was about to say something. She put her index finger on his lips. "Not a word. Not a sound," she breathed, with butterfly softness. For a moment, he saw her smooth, perfect body. She slid his pajama bottoms to his knees. Then she pulled him down, deep into her.

It took less than a minute. Way less. Maybe ten seconds. Lewis whispered, "I'm sorry, I..." and she again put her finger to his lips, then raised her head to kiss him, then laid back down and put her finger on his lips again.

"I have to go," she said. "Sweet dreams." She rolled him off her and stood up.

Lewis climbed into his bed and passed out.

Chapter Five: The morning after

"Hey, Lew, get up." Ted banged on the door and went in. "Get up, man. Mom's making breakfast."

"Ted, it's..." and he looked at his phone. "Oh, it's nine o'clock. Okay. Gotta get up some time."

"Good morning, boys," Jill said, as she poured pancake batter over the banana slices and pecan halves already sizzling in the peanut oil in the red copper pan. "I hope you're hungry."

"Mom, we had a huge dinner. But well, I love your banana-pecan pancakes. Lew, did you ever try those?"

"That's a southern recipe. Yeah, but I had 'em in Chicago. Lou Mitchell's. 'Southern,' right. I love them. Thanks, Miss Jill."

"Coffee's already made. Anybody need anything, or do you just drink it black?"

"Black for me, thank you," Lewis said.

"So, did you sleep all right?" as she brought a huge stack of pancakes and placed it on the table. "Dig in. Syrup's right here," and she pulled a white glass pitcher, maybe a pint, out of the beeping microwave.

"I slept like I was dead," Ted said. I don't even remember getting into bed."

"You, Lewis? Do you remember getting into bed, or did you just fall asleep, too?"

He squirmed a bit, but recovered. "I had a real good night, Miss Jill, thank you."

As she cleared the table, Jill said, "What do you have planned for today, anything? Got all your Christmas shopping done already?"

"I'm sending cards to a few people, letters to even less," Lewis said, "so I guess I'm done. But isn't today the worst day to go shopping?"

"Bargains," Ted said, "as if students had any money, anyway." They all laughed. "Actually, though, Bill Winter is building a boat in his garage, and he asked me if I wanted to see it, so I'm going over there after lunch. I've got some studying to do this morning, if that's all okay. Lew, you want to come with me? Bill's cool. We went to high school together."

"Well, I guess I'll study this morning, too. If I make any progress, sure, that'd be neat. Sure."

* * *

"Hi, Mom," Ted said as he came into the living room two hours later. "Thanks for everything. I just wanted to say thanks. I love you, Mom."

"Thank you, Ted. It's so nice to hear. You never used to say that, when you were younger. Not for maybe ten years. It's good to hear it again. You're growing up, aren't you?"

"I'm... Mom, truth? I'm lonely. I'm confused. There's so much different, living away. It's good. I mean, I have to do it some time, right? But it's weird. Everybody's new. Everybody's so serious about getting grades, and it's not like high school.

"I mean, I used to always be... I don't want to sound like bragging, but I mean, you know, I was pretty much always the smartest kid in my class, or at least right up there. But here? Everybody was the smartest kid in their class. It's like I'm trying really hard, and I'm just average. It's weird. And there's nobody I know, nobody I've known more than a couple months. My new friends, Lewis, they're great, but it's not the same as when I lived here, where I knew everybody from grade school or high school, kids I've known my whole life. It's..."

"It's growing up. And no, it doesn't get easier. You just learn to adapt to new people, new things, sometimes too fast to be comfortable. And you don't get time to really know your new friends, either. Somebody seems just fine, then you find out they were using you. Or some guy you thought was your friend, he takes your girlfriend, or he takes something from your dorm room. Just steals it. And when you talk to him, he doesn't even care. It happens. Bad things happen, a lot, and those friends you don't really know, they turn out not to be your friends, sometimes. The quicker you learn to read them, the more skills you develop – whom to trust, whom to watch – the better you learn that, that's going to be more important than most of that stuff in your books, even your chemistry books.

"But you're going to get hurt, betrayed even. And you haven't even mentioned a girlfriend yet."

"Nothing to report there, Mom, but I'll keep you posted. Saw a girl named Jessica a couple times, but both of us are too busy getting grades right now. Maybe next semester, when half my class flunks out, I'll have a better chance. Right now, the party kids all hang out together. Some of them won't be back. Maybe I'll spend a little more time…"

"Maybe she will, too." Jill smiled. "So are you and Lewis going to look at Bill's boat?"

"I will. I haven't seen Lewis since breakfast. Maybe. Speaking of lunch..."

"Were we speaking of lunch? How can you be hungry? I'll make some turkey sandwiches. That okay?"

"That'd be great, Mom. Thanks."

"Go get your roommate. Lunch in ten minutes."

* * *

"Lewis?" Ted banged on the door. "Lunch. Wash up."

"Okay," and he came out, headed to the bathroom. "I'll be right there. "

Jill had set out plates, sandwiches, and some cans of soda from the fridge. "Sit down and enjoy your second turkey meal in twenty-four hours."

"It was great last night, Miss Jill," Lewis said, "and it looks just as good now. Yes," he nodded to Ted, "save me a dark meat. Thanks."

Jill said, "So, Ted, are you and Lewis headed over to Bill Winter's?"

"I don't know. Lew, wanna go?"

"How long will it take?"

"He's half an hour away, so maybe two hours."

Lewis looked at Ted, then at Jill. She smiled. "Man, that's a lot of time. I mean... I really got a lot of studying to do. Can you shoot me some pictures?"

"Well, okay. It's not like he knows you or anything. So I might be longer. Is that okay, Mom?"

"There's weather coming in tonight, Ted. It might snow, so if you're going be any more than two hours, call me, okay? And be home by five, no matter what. It gets dark so early."

"Sure, Mom. I'll call you when I leave, no matter if it's early or late."

"That's fine, Ted. Have fun, and say hello to Bill for me."

"See ya," said Lewis, and he dove onto his second sandwich.

* * *

Ted was on the road to Bill's, and Lewis helped clean up and put dishes away. "Do you really have that much studying to do?" Jill asked.

"Some."

"Can it wait?" She kissed him.

He nodded. "I guess it can wait." Again, she led him to the guest room, but this time, she pulled back the sheets and closed the blinds and locked the door behind them.

"Why'd you lock the door?" Lewis asked.

"Atmosphere," she said, and unbuttoned his shirt.

He started to pull her sweater up, and she slapped his hands away. "*When* I say, and *if* I say," she said. "Only then will you touch me. Understand?"

"Yes, Miss Jill." and she undressed him all the way and pushed him lightly onto the bed.

"Now, you fold my clothes as I hand them to you. Do you understand?" He nodded.

She pulled off her sweater, nothing underneath, and she tossed it into the corner of the room. Lewis sat, gaze fixed on her breasts. "Well, *fold* it," she said.

He stood up awkwardly, his cock leading the way, picked up her sweater, turned around, and she was naked, standing like a statue of some gifted sculptor's vision of a perfect woman, the dimmed light passing through the blinds and side-lighting her. Again, he just stood there.

"Are you going to fold that?"

"Wha, where do you want me to put it?"

"Just hand it to me," she said, and she threw it on top of her jeans, in the corner. "Come here," and she put her arms around his waist and drew him to her. He almost lost his balance, took baby steps. "Just, right here, where we're standing," and she put one hand behind his waist, held the back of his neck with her other. She was short. He was tall, so she walked him to the bed and had him lie on his back as she joined him.

"You're not in charge here," she said, as she reared back. And he came.

"I – I'm sorry, Miss Jill."

"You're new to this," she said. "Practice makes perfect. You just need practice. Lots and lots of practice." She stood up, pulled on her jeans and sweater, and walked out. He started to follow. "No. Stay here. You have a lot of studying to do, remember?"

Lewis looked around, found his clothes, put them back on, and sat back down on the bed. *What the hell am I doing?*

* * *

He made notes on three new chapters. *I need a break. What's in the kitchen?* He was looking in the fridge for a can of pop when Ted called Jill's phone.

"I'm going to be another hour, if that's all right," he said. "That would still get me home by six. Would that work, Mom?"

"Sure, Ted, but call me if you're going to be any later." She put the phone down, turned to Lewis, and said, "Come with me."

Lewis went immediately down the hall to his room, blinds still drawn. Jill took her clothes off first, slowly, and handed them to him to fold and put on the desk. Then she pulled his shirt up over his head, stopping with his arms up. He couldn't see. She unbuttoned his pants, pulled them down to the floor and left them around his ankles. His shirt was still holding up his arms when she tipped him backwards onto the bed and she licked the top of his cock, just a little. He started to quiver.

"Don't move," she said, and backed away. She ran her hand up between his thighs, slower and slower as she went. He was shaking. "Stop. Relax. Breathe. Breathe very slowly." She climbed over him, straddling him just above his knees, his arms still over his head, his eyes still blinded by his shirt. She moved up to bring the two of them together, took charge of him,... and he came. All over his own stomach, all over her hand. He fought to get the shirt off. Jill stayed right there.

"I suppose this may take more practice," she said, as she stood up and went to the desk to get her jeans and sweater. "Either you'll learn, or I'll just have to keep training you."

"I'm sorry, Miss Jill. This never happened before. I mean, since the first time."

"You've never been with a woman, have you?"

He looked shocked. "That's *all* I've been with. What do you mean?"

"I mean, you've been with *girls*. Have you ever been with an older woman?"

He did his best to act indignant. "Yes, in fact. Kathy. She's a senior."

"Lewis, she's a girl. If you're going to be with a *woman*, you're going to have to become a man. And it takes practice, hard work." They both smiled. "Are you willing to work, work hard, to learn what it takes?"

He nodded, grinning like a little kid at his own surprise birthday party.

"Then go take a shower, and don't get that all over the bed. Ted's coming home, so straighten up here and get back to your books."

"Yes, Miss Jill."

* * *

"Hey, Lew, didn't you get my pictures? I texted 'em to you. Did you see Bill's boat?"

"Oh, uh, no, Ted. Sorry. I had the phone off. Took a little nap after I did some biology. Just got up and took a shower. Let's see this boat."

* * *

The skies were gloomy, the trees featureless grey skeletons on the hour-long trip back to school. They approached the dorm. "So sorry you boys have to leave," Jill said. "I really enjoyed having you. You're gone, the house is pretty quiet. In some ways, that's nice, but I miss having someone to talk to."

"Mom, I really appreciate your doing all the work, getting us home and back, and wow, I never realized how much I love your cooking."

"Yes, thank you, Miss Jill. I really enjoyed the weekend. You were great."

"Thank you, Ted." She turned. "And Lewis, will you come again?"

"I'd sure like to. Thanks again."

As they went into their dorm room Saturday afternoon, everything was the same as when they left. Except Lewis. Lewis was different.

Chapter Six: Jack's big caper

Jill fumbled for the ringing phone in her purse, swerving half a lane into oncoming traffic. Except there was no oncoming traffic. "Hi, Jack... yes, the boys are gone... Yes, he's growing up... I'm exhausted... Well, I could use a little help cleaning up, laundry... Jack, I'm tired... Well, okay, hate to waste a Sunday. I'll see you in a couple. I'll be home in half an hour... See you about seven, then."

Jill had one set of bedding in the wash, the other already in the dryer, when Jack saw the front door ajar and let himself in. "Baby doll," he said, as he walked toward her, arms open and a huge smile on his face. "Now I know what I'm thankful for." Big hug.

"Hi, honey. Did you have a good Thanksgiving? Would you want the last turkey sandwich of the season? Some sweet potatoes, maybe?"

"Anything at all, sweetheart. I probably don't need to eat for three more days, but I love being fussed over, and I love everything you do for me. So, sure. I brought some nice bourbon. I'll get the ice?"

"Yes, go ahead. About three fingers for me. I didn't have a drop of anything with the boys here."

"Boys? Plural?"

"Ted brought his roommate."

"What's he like?

"Nice boy. Typical. They were either hanging out together, getting thrown out of the old prison by the police, or studying. Or eating." She laughed.

"Some things never change." He laughed, too, sat on the living room couch. "I got caught when I was about sixteen, climbing the water tower back in Dayton. It was Thanksgiving, come to think of it. Three of us got up there. Dave, Tony, and I, we were so nuts. It was almost dark. All we wanted to do was get back down. Those metal ladder steps, they're cold, and it's windy up there. We were freezing, and our hands were numb. We just got started coming down, about ten feet from the top, when the cops showed up. Suddenly, it was bright. Big-ass spotlight right on us. We were so busted."

"What happened?"

"Well, they waited for us to get to the bottom. Then they marched us to the police car, made us sit on the back seat."

"Handcuffs, Miranda, all that?"

"Naw. Just warmed us up in the back seat. We were shivering something awful, and our hands were all torn up. But they acted real tough. Threatened to call our parents. That would have been worse than jail."

"So what did you do?"

"After we warmed up and they had said all the threatening stuff they could think of, they told us if they caught us up there again, they'd shoot us down. But this time, they just wanted us to go home, and never sin again."

"So *that* was your big caper? That's the worst trouble you ever got into?"

"I'm afraid so." He gave a sheepish look. "It seemed like a bigger deal at the time."

"Did you sin again?"

"None of us ever climbed a water tower again, anyway." He reached out. "Here's your drink. But now that you mention it, I wouldn't mind sinning again, a little, if you're up for it."

"Let's eat first. Maybe watch a movie."

* * *

Dawn came late, the Sunday after Thanksgiving. Jill opened her eyes, groggy. Jack had snored, loud, most of the night. *At least he fell asleep after one go.* "Wake up, Jack, it's morning. There's going to be bacon and eggs on the table in a few minutes."

"Oh, honey. Thanks. You were wonderful last night. Sorry I was so tired, hope I didn't disappoint you."

"Never, Jack. Just go get yourself a shower and I'll see you in the kitchen."

"I don't know how you do it."

I don't even know why I do it, sometimes. "It's because I like taking care of my big ol' teddy bear. But let's have the orange juice this morning, no vodka. That bourbon last night was potent, and I had too much." *Or maybe not enough. Oh, he's nice enough, even if he's no dynamo. But he loves me, sort of, and I love him, I guess. And he takes care of things now and then. The brakes and tires – that was nice, and that really helped, a lot. He can't help it he's old and snores.*

"Okay baby, all cleaned up. I'm a new man." He crossed the kitchen and gave her a big kiss, and she liked it.

"Sit down, Jack." She pulled out his chair at the kitchen table. "I've been slingin' grits all morning, just waitin' for a truckin' man to walk in and appreciate 'em."

"I – I'm not a trucker." Confused.

"Oh, hell, Jack. Sit down. I was just playing 'Maybelle, the Queen of the Diner.' And there's no grits, either. Have some bacon?"

"He laughed. "Dense in the morning. And yes, I do believe I'd like a couple of those crispy little nitrosamine sticks. How can anything so good be so bad for you?"

"Sometimes, that's how you know it's bad for you – how good it seems." *Wow, that's the truth, isn't it, Jill? Lewis never had a chance. Gave him one. Well, more like half a dozen chances. Quick learner. Well, attentive, anyway...*

"Jill, you in there?"

"Oh, sorry. Lost in thought. I really liked having Ted home, even for a couple days. Makes me feel old, alone, now that he's gone again."

"Honey, you're not old, and you'll never be alone. You've got me."

"For last night, for today, anyway... Jack, what are we doing?"

"You mean, ...us? What are we doing together, or what are we doing this afternoon?"

"You know what I mean. Do we have a future? Do we make plans? Do we just keep doing this – seeing each other on weekends, sneaking around Ted? Having fun, being nice to each other? But what then? What now, even?"

"What now? I love you, Jill. I don't know where this will go. I'm taking it slow. The divorce is so recent, I, I don't know if I have the confidence to get into another permanent relationship so soon. I know I love you, though. That, I know."

"So soon? Jack, it's been two years since Cheryl moved out."

"Yes, but only since summer we've been divorced. There's a difference."

"How? How is there a difference? She moved out. You didn't have anything to do with each other. You communicated through lawyers. You never saw each other, except in court. You haven't seen, or even talked to her in a year, right? How is that different?"

"Jill, I don't know. I've never had a spouse die, but it's different from divorce. With a divorce, they're gone, but they're still around. They're not *gone*. Does that make any sense to you?"

"Jack," she cradled his head and pulled him to her. They kissed. "I don't know, either. I've never been divorced. Maybe it is different. I guess we both don't know what it's like for each other. Sorry."

"Let's not worry about it, honey. Let's just take it as it comes. When we know,… we'll know."

"Both of us?"

"Both of us."

"Okay."

"I love you."

"You have to go home."

Chapter Seven: Nicole

Ted and Jessica's attraction worked two ways in the chemistry lab. Both were serious about their major. Both had been top students in high school chemistry, and now both were ascending to the top of their class. Studying together was synergistic; there wasn't any competition between them. But the attraction was building up in the background, getting harder to ignore, or hide. Sometimes they'd fall asleep together in the Union, studying on a couch. "You think it's like this, when old married people are used to each other?" she asked.

"I hope so, but I hope it isn't over a chemistry book."

Lewis spent until midterms looking for Nicole, and he saw her one Tuesday night, heading for her dorm after that nine o'clock class was out. "Carry your books?" he said, as she smiled, said nothing, and handed them over, walking fast.

"Busy tonight?" he said, trying to watch where he was going and still look at her face, getting distracted by her soft black leather jacket that was maybe a size too small.

"I'm busy walking to my dorm," she said, "and I'm busy wondering what excuse you're going to give me for not calling all this time."

"No excuse. I just didn't know your schedule, or where you lived, or your last name. And you ran off with your girlfriend without giving me your email or phone number."

"You didn't wait for me to come back out."

"I didn't know how long you'd take, and… oh, screw it. Do you want to go out?"

She stopped walking. "Go out, or screw?"

"Either?"

"Both."

"Okay."

Nicole had a girlfriend who lived off-campus and went home on weekends, and she gave Nicole a key, "to watch her plants." She also had evening classes Mondays and Thursdays. For the next three weeks, Nicole and Lewis made sure that the plants were happy.

"You don't talk much," she said, as they took a break one night.

"I'm listening to your desires," Lewis said, and Nicole stuck her finger down her throat, mock-gagging herself.

"How about, we have to give her some money for all this booze of hers that we're drinking?"

"I can do that," he said.

"And how about, you fuck me one more time and we get out of here before she gets home?"

"That, too." She got up, pony style, and he did the stallion thing. Neither paid too much attention to the noise her head was making against the wall, until the doorbell rang.

"Hey, knock it off in there, or try a quieter position or something. I'm trying to study."

They were finished, anyway.

She said, "I think you hurt my head."

"Sorry, I was kinda lost in the moment. I'll chip in for some aspirin, too."

She smiled. "Get outta here. See you tomorrow?"

* * *

"Say, Nicole, now that we're getting to know each other better, can I ask you a personal question?"

"The worst I can say is go fuck yourself."

"Well, okay. I, uhhh… So, the night we met, you were with your friends?"

"I just hang with them once in a while. They're not my friends."

"Fine. Well, one of them told my roommate that you're a ball buster. That true?"

"I don't know. Depends. Are your balls okay?"

"Well, uh, yeah, I guess so. But what were they talking about?"

"It was just two nights before I met you," she started. "Here, sit down. First week of school, I met this guy. Hot, but flakey, you know what I mean?"

Lewis nodded. He didn't have a clue, but this wasn't the time to ask for a definition.

"We went out, he got buzzed, we came back here, started making out, pretty slow. I like to get to know guys before I have sex."

Lewis nodded again. *Maybe a few minutes, anyway…*

"So this guy? He pushes me down on the bed. We were upstairs, right here, where we are now."

"Yeah?" Lewis wondered if she was ever going to get to the good part.

"He pushes me down, actually ripped my shirt. I said, 'Hey, asshole, get outta here,' but he starts getting fresh, and I know, like, I can't *talk* him out of it."

"Asshole, " Lewis said. "So, what'd you do?"

"You know those real nice jeans I have, zip up the sides so I can get my feet through?"

He remembered. He smiled. "Those super-tight ones?"

"Yeah. Well, I had those on, and I'm afraid maybe he's going to rip those, too, so I say, 'Look, at least let me take these jeans off. I don't want you to tear 'em,' and he goes like, okay."

"Real gentleman. He's already torn your shirt, and you're taking your pants off for him *voluntarily?*"

"Just let me finish, okay? Shut up, Lew… So, he's taking off his pants, has 'em down around his ankles. He's about to step out of 'em, but he's sweaty, and the idiot's left his shoes on, so he can't get the jeans off. His dick's hanging out there, he's trying to get his jeans off his ankles, I'm taking off my stilettoes. Can you see that picture?"

"I guess."

"So, he's got his feet tangled up in his jeans at the ankles, and I take off my shoes, and I start hitting him with the heel, as hard as I can, shouting at him. I hit him on the head, on his neck, all over his back. A couple holes – he's bleeding a couple places, and I'm beating on him as hard as I can with the heel, *screaming* at him. He's hopping down the stairs, feet still tangled up in the jeans." She was laughing. So was Lewis.

"And he's screaming for help, feet stuck together as he falls out the front door, cock dangling in the air, hands trying to get his feet free, and he falls on his face down the front stairs, yelling for help, and I'm still hitting him as hard as I can."

Lewis was laughing his ass off. "What happened? Did he get away?"

"No, the neighbors – you know them, they hear everything, I guess – they called the cops, and the cops showed up. He's lying on the grass out by the sidewalk, trying to pull his pants back on. By this time, *all* the neighbors are watching. The cops look at me, say, 'Miss, you all right?' and I say, 'Now I am.' Asshole's still lying on the ground, hurting. Cop says, 'Miss, you go inside. We'll take it from here.' So that's what I did."

"He didn't file charges?"

"Would *you?* All beat up by the girl he was trying to rape?"

Lew grunted as he zipped up his jeans. "Okay, so I know you're dangerous in those heels. I always thought you were, but now I know." Then he said, "That's funny, though."

* * *

Still smiling the following Sunday morning, but his mood was changed. "Nicole, I'm really having fun with you. You can see that." She nodded, serious now, too. "And don't get me wrong, I really love what we're doing. But I'm wondering, some time, you want to study a little? I mean, I'm behind a couple chapters on my English lit anthology. We could, you know, read together a little."

She lost the smile. "I don't want to read with you, Lewis. I want to fuck. That's all I want to do, all weekend. And drink."

"How about…?"

"That's *all* I want to do, Lewis."

"Then you're going to have to do it by yourself. I've got to study, and this weekend is it for me."

"You owe me thirty bucks for her booze."

He pulled out two twenties from his wallet in his pants on the floor, dropped them on the bed. "Keep the change. See you next semester, if you make it back. I hope you get fucked. Good luck."

Chapter Eight: Jack Claus

Three weeks and a few days after dropping Ted and Lewis off in Columbus, Jill was headed back. *Ted and me, Christmas, like when he was a child. But no Andy. It won't be the same. Jack was right. We're not divorced. Andy's gone. really gone. Forever.* She cried a bit, private tears.

She called Jack. "Hi... Yeah, I'm driving to school.... A long time... Monday, the week after New Year's... Yes, that's why I called. I'd like you to visit for a couple days, meet Ted, say the day after Christmas, maybe spend two nights? ...*Yes*, in the guest room... Okay, good. We'll talk before then, but Merry Christmas, Jack."

* * *

"Hi, Mom." They met in the dorm lobby. He was waiting, all packed. He hugged her. "Merry Christmas."

"Ted." She hugged him, suddenly feeling deep emotion. Her son, the person she cared about more than anything, was going to be home for four weeks. She pulled herself together, and he never noticed. "Can't wait to get you home. You have all your books, everything you need? You ready?"

"I'm so ready to get out of this place, Mom. I mean, I love it and all, but I want to be back home. You, my friends, good food..." They both laughed.

"Is Lewis...?"

"He's already left, about an hour ago. Heading down to Chillicothe. Won't see his ugly mug for a month, either." And they laughed again.

* * *

On Christmas morning, Ted slept in 'til almost nine. When he snuck out to the living room, he looked under the little fake tree, the one they had used every year for the past ten, and there was a three-car train.

Crayon-colored shoe boxes, with little paper details taped on – a cab on the black steam engine, a lookout tower on the red caboose. Bright blue wheels – he never did know why he made them blue – on all. Ted looked at it, picked it up, looked at his mother, tears in his eyes.

"Mom, where did that come from? I made that in kindergarten. You saved it? Where did you hide it?"

She looked at him as he held the shoe-box engine with bright blue wheels. Her five-year-old, now all grown up, with tears in his eyes. "I just kept it for the right time. And this seemed like the right time. You don't remember, but you wanted a train set, and I was so broke."

"I do remember. You said if I wanted a train set, why didn't I make one – then it could be just the way I wanted it. It was, too. It was perfect. You were so smart."

He cried in earnest now, looking at the clouds of smoke he had drawn on the top of the box, behind the smokestack. The smokestack was in different places on each side and the top, but it was there, and the smoke made it authentic.

He set it on the coffee table and hugged his mom. "That's the best Christmas present ever. You're the best mom ever. I love you so much."

They hugged and cried together, she always the mom, he on his way to a new universe.

"Here, Mom. This is for you." He handed her a card, with a hand-written letter inside.

Dear Mom,

Merry Christmas. I love you. I never realized how much you did for me when I was a kid, all the things I never noticed. I was always warm in the winter. I always had shoes that fit, good food.

My life was really easy, but I didn't know it. I'm sorry I complained when I had to help around the house. I didn't know how much there was to do, and I didn't see why I should have to empty the garbage or mow the lawn or help with the dishes. Guess I figured my room cleaned itself, too.

But everything is different when I'm away, and I can see it. Sure, somebody feeds me, but they don't care about me. They teach me stuff, but it's their job.

*I have friends, but they don't love me.
I get advice whenever I need it, but I
don't know if it's good, or if they're
maybe up to something. I ask questions,
but I don't know if they're telling me
the truth when they answer.*

*You, everything you do, I believe in
you. You always have my back, my best in-
terests at heart. I can trust you, believe in you completely. I trust my
roommate with my wallet - I leave it
around the room, but you, Mom, I trust
you with my soul.*

*I love you, and finally I understand
what that means, deep down.*

Merry Christmas.

Your son,

Ted

"That's beautiful, Ted. Thank you so much. And I'll always love you, more than anything else in the world. Merry Christmas."

* * *

Breakfast was coffee, toast, and jam. Ted cleaned up and did the dishes without being asked, then said, "Mom, if you don't need me for a while, I think I'll go study, get ahead on next term. That okay?"

Smiling. "Well, if you're through playing with your train set for a while, I guess so." And her phone rang as Ted headed down the hall.

She recognized the caller and adopted a fake formal air. "Merry Christmas. Hamlin residence. Jill Hamlin speaking."

"Merry Christmas, cupcake. Jack Pope here. How are you?"

"Fine, Jack. What are you doing for Christmas?"

"I thought I'd come over this evening, bring a present, love a certain lady..."

"Ted's here, you know. Guest room only."

"Well, okay. I can make it by five, if that'll work for you."

"Sure. There's plenty of food. But be careful. There's supposed to be a nasty storm rolling in."

"I will. I can bring something, too. Do you need anything?"

"No, just yourself. And be careful. I want my teddy bear safe and warm for Christmas."

"If it looks like I'll be late, I'll call. Can't wait to see you. Merry Christmas."

* * *

Ted emerged from his room about two o'-clock, hunger finally overcoming his desire to read more "stupid general ed books."

"Hi, Mom. I don't want to sound like I'm nagging, but... when's dinner?"

"Plan on around seven. You have plenty of time. I'll fix you something. Mac and cheese? Soup? Sandwich?"

"You don't have to make it, Mom. I'll just..."

"You'll just find the one thing I need for tonight, and eat it. You're blessed that way. No, hey – how about a grilled cheese?"

"That'd be perfect, Mom. Thank you. And is there any coffee left?"

"Now *that* you can make, yourself."

He brewed ten cups and took a thermos and another full cup to his room, where he quickly devoured his next chapter of chemistry.

* * *

The snow started around four, and by dark, an hour later, there was a blizzard going on. Not cold, in the twenties. But the first big snow of the year, big fat flakes, and it accumulated fast. Crews weren't keeping up. Local television and radio had their cub reporters out in the mess, shouting their reports from the side of the road, a foot or two from where the blinded snowplow drivers had to go. Jill had the television on, the little one on the kitchen counter.

Stations must hate their newest reporters. They're always sending those kids out. "Here's what a hurricane looks like," they say. "Stay indoors – this kind of blizzard can kill you," they say. "Tornadoes are all over the area. Take immediate cover," they say, and some film crew is out there, waiting for someone – maybe themselves – to be killed. Great for ratings, eh?

And these kids, right out of journalism school, giving us advice? We can see they're idiots, out in that weather. Why would we take their advice about anything?

Her phone rang. "Hi, Jack. Oh, Jack, are you all right? It's snowing like crazy here. Are you on the road?"

"Hi, baby. Yes, I'm about half an hour out. I've been on one road or another for three hours. As soon as I get going, there's another wreck, another detour, another road closed. What're we supposed to do, just stop in the middle of nowhere and freeze to death? 'You can't go on – it's too dangerous,' they say. 'Yeah, well, it's just as dangerous where I came from, three stinking hours ago, and it's three hours back and one hour forward. So, arrest me,' I said to the last guy."

"Jack, they're just doing their job."

"And I'm coming to see my baby. Let's see who's more motivated, huh? I really should hang up and drive, though. Half an hour, forty-five minutes, tops. Can you wait that long for me?"

"You know where to find me. Be safe. I want my big ol' teddy bear here in one piece tonight."

"See you, doll. I gotta drive now."

* * *

The new snow was half a foot deep, drifting three times that, and building fast when the doorbell rang at seven-thirty. Ted answered it.

"Hi. I'm Jack Pope." He pulled the glove off his right hand, extended it, shook Ted's.

"I'm Ted. Come on in."

Jack stomped off the extra snow from his shiny shoes and closed the door behind him. Jill came out from the kitchen. "Hi, Jack. Merry Christmas. So glad you could get here. All this snow!"

"It's coming this way. I've been in it, trying to break through the front, since I left Dayton. It's going to be a beast." Jack picked up a sack he had brought in his left hand, and pulled out two wrapped presents. "The big one's for you, Ted," he said, "and the little one's for your mother."

"Mom, you got a bottle of something. But let's open after dinner, like, you know, tradition." He turned. "Thanks, Mister Pope. Nice to meet you. Merry Christmas."

Jill said, "Into the kitchen, guys. The little round table's not very formal, but it's cozy, and it's closest to the food."

Jack said, "It's great to finally be here, to meet you, Ted. The roads weren't all that bad, but it's like everybody forgot how to drive in snow. And every time we'd start moving, some moron would decide to go fifteen miles an hour, and make the guy behind him go into a skid, trying to slow down – or some maniac would try to go sixty, like it was a dry road. I had two of those guys who passed me like that – I saw one of them in the ditch later."

"And everybody who went your speed," Ted said, "was perfectly safe and rational." Jill shot him a glance, but he kept going. "How did you pick the perfect speed?"

Jack laughed, irritated but smiling. "Well, you got me on that, son, but there's a wide range of safe and sane speeds. The good driver picks a speed somewhere in that range, and adjusts to the other drivers, the road itself… all that stuff." He knew he sounded like a Driver's Ed tape. He shrugged and looked at Jill, who gave Ted a disparaging glance that the student didn't see.

"Ready?" she said. "I hope you're hungry." She set the green beans, mashed potatoes and gravy, and her specialty, meat loaf, on the table. "Everybody has water. Anybody want anything else?"

"Mom, water's fine. Just sit down, relax. Join us. You've been working on Christmas non-stop. Just enjoy it with us."

"The boy's right, Jill. All we want here is you. Everything's perfect."

After dinner, everyone retired to the living room. Jill gave Jack an elaborately-wrapped bottle of cologne, and she unwrapped her Maker's Mark, feigning surprise.

Ted's turn. He again thanked Jack and since there wasn't any card, tore into the big box. In it was another box, gift-wrapped. Inside that was a lot of crumpled newsprint and a small box. "Hamilton," it said, and inside was a black-dial Jazzmaster watch.

"Oh, man," Ted said. "Thank you, Mister Pope. Thank you so much. This is fantastic."

"Jack, it's gorgeous, but you shouldn't have. You *really* shouldn't have," and Jill meant it.

"I know nobody needs a watch any more. Everybody's got a phone. But that makes a watch more special – it's a statement." And to Ted, "It's 'Jack,' and it's good for, like two miles under the ocean."

"Thanks, Jack. It'll be 'specially useful if I'm ever drowning and I need to know what time it is."

They both laughed. Jill continued her glare at Jack.

"What I'm saying… if you get caught in a rainstorm, it won't get wrecked. You can wear it all the time."

"Oh, I will. I will. I'll *sleep* with it on."

"It doesn't do all that fancy stuff – alarm, monitor your heartbeat, predict solar eclipses… there's apps for all that stuff. It just gives you the time at a glance. Date, if you don't know it."

"It's great, Jack. Thank you very much."

Jill said, "Now back to studying," and Ted bowed out, wearing his new watch and taking the box with him.

"Merry Christmas, everybody." His bedroom door closed behind him.

Jill tried to whisper, but it was more like a hiss. "Jack, what the hell are you up to? A *thousand-dollar watch?* What's the matter with you?"

He remained calm. "I wanted the kid to like me. That's all."

"He would have liked you anyway. You could have brought him a coloring book or pajamas, and he would have liked you. A thousand-dollar *watch?*"

"More like six hundred. Anyway, crayons can mess up your laundry."

"Oh, you," and she pushed him to the floor and planted a big kiss on his lips. "Come with me, you big…"

* * *

Jill kicked Jack out of her room after about twenty minutes, all done for the night. "Tomorrow is another day, Jack. Be ready."

"Yes, ma'am." He winked at her as he turned out the light. Then he quietly shut the door and went down the hall to the guest room with the squeaky bed.

He's a lot older than he looks, I guess. And he isn't getting any younger. Would he be insulted if I offered him a blue pill? Oh, god – what if he's already taking it? Now I'm insulting myself.

Jill thought about Lewis, with his always-on cock. *But he can't just take it slow. Not yet, anyway. But who cares? He's ready again in ten minutes.* Jill shut down her consciousness and fell asleep.

* * *

Ted was up making coffee at seven. Jill heard him, pulled on her bathrobe, and joined him in the kitchen, started making toast, getting the grape jam out of the fridge.

"Sleep okay, Ted?"

"I stayed up a little, reading the watch instructions."

"How much instruction do you need for an electric watch that has no functions?"

"I was trying to read the instructions in all the languages, Mom. It's like a Rosetta Stone. I know what it says, so I look at the other languages and see if I can figure out which word is which."

"Can you?"

"Mostly. Not Russian. And really not Chinese and Japanese and Korean. And Arabic, or whatever that is."

"Toast's ready."

Ted poured two coffees. He and his mom sat down. And Jack said a brief hi on his way to the bathroom. "If there's any coffee…" he said.

"We got it for you," Ted shouted, as the bathroom door closed.

Jill started more toast. "Do you think you'd like some eggs?"

"Let's wait until he's out. Maybe he wants to see a restaurant," Ted said, with a sparkle in his eye.

Jill was buttering Jack's toast as he pulled out the third chair at the round table. "Thanks, baby," he said, pulling his coffee and toast nearer. "Say, would you and the boy want to join me for breakfast somewhere here in town? Do you have some favorite spot?"

Ted said, "Mom, could we go to Blackbird?"

Jack said, "Can you sit down there?"

"It's this bakery in a coffee shop. Great coffee, too." Jack turned to Jill, and she continued. "Can't get out of there for less than a thousand calories, but it's worth it. Oh, those cinnamon buns!"

"Can we bring home a pie, too?" Ted said. "Remember when you asked what I miss at school? Well, that's my new answer and I'm sticking to it."

"Let's go," Jack said. He looked at Ted. "You navigate. I'll drive."

Ten minutes past toast, Ted was sitting shotgun in Jack's black Buick SUV. The snow crunched, packing as they backed out of the drive. "Sorry, Mom, I'll shovel when we get back, okay?" Jill nodded. Ted said to himself, *black Buick SUV?*

* * *

The coffee house said "Relax" on the sign, but the noise – all the happy talking, half of Mansfield was there – kept anybody from saying much, or at least from hearing much.

On the ride home, Ted said, "Thanks, Jack. Great breakfast, and thanks for the pie. That'll be great with dinner." When they got to the driveway, he said, "Stop here in the street for a few minutes, and I'll get this shoveled out. Snow's stopped and we've got some sun. It'll dry off in half an hour, be good as new."

Jack and Jill went up the hill and into the house. Jill opened the garage door, Ted got the shovel, and cleared the drive in ten minutes. He stomped off the snow, kicked off his shoes, and went into the kitchen. There was a cup of cold coffee still in the carafe. He poured it into his cup and set the microwave for one minute. "The driveway will be dry any time. Do you want me to pull your SUV in off the street, Mister Pope?"

"Thanks, son, but it's 'Jack,'" he said, as he tossed Ted the keys.

Ted came back inside, said "All set," to Jack. *Son? You presumptuous asshole.* Ted tossed the keys back to him, just a touch faster than comfortable, but barely noticeable. He grabbed his coffee out of the beeping micro and went to his room. *Son? Who the hell is he, anyway?*

Chemistry lost its charm in a few minutes, and Ted felt like taking a nap. Jill woke him, two hours later. "Do you want to come join us for some pie à la mode?"

Ted took his place at the round table, a hot quarter of a pie under two scoops of ice cream waiting for him.

Jack said, "I see you're still wearing the watch. Do you like it, son?"

Ted cringed, but said in a normal tone, "It's very nice, Mister Pope. Thank you."

"Call me Jack."

"Sure. Thank you, Jack." Quiet for a moment as everybody dug in.

When there was a bite and a half left on Ted's plate, he noticed Jack's hand on his leg. Ted moved, pushed the chair out a little. The hand went away. *Mistake. I'm just too jumpy. Gotta give this guy the benefit of the doubt. Mom likes him, and it is a really nice watch. Don't want to make a scene.*

And the hand was back, insistently, and higher on Ted's leg. *No mistake.* "Thanks Mom," and he went to his room and closed the door.

Ted locked the door. He wanted to take a shower, felt dirty. *But Mom likes him. He's her boyfriend. I'll never see him again, anyway. It's not for me to spoil it for her. And what if it is just a mistake? Yeah, but it's no mistake. That perv was grabbing my leg. Yuk. So what am I going to do about it?*

Ted fell asleep again. Sometimes his mind cleared just before sleep took over.

Jill knocked on his door, then turned the knob and realized it was locked. "Ted, are you all right?"

"Yeah, Mom. Just tired."

"Jack's gone home, and I still have some pie and ice cream. Care for a healthy supper?"

"Apple pie?" and he opened the door.

"…and meat loaf, not in that order. Come sit down with me and tell me what's on your mind."

"Nothing, Mom," as he pulled out her chair. I've just got a lot to do, and I'm feeling like I should get it done, and I'm not doing it."

"Overwhelmed?"

"A little."

"It's not Jack, is it?"

"Mom, Jack is your business."

"You don't like him? I mean, that watch…"

"It's a great watch, Mom. But I don't need a watch. I don't have to like him, do I? I mean, I know you do, and all, but,…"

"No, Ted. I'd like it if you two would get along. Maybe you'll like him, once you get to know him. He's trying awful hard."

"Yeah, I know. I don't know. Maybe I'll get to like him, I guess. Like I said, he's your business. I'll be gone most of the time from now on, anyway…"

"Oh, Ted, don't say that! You still have three and a half more years of college, maybe grad school,…"

"And I'll get married and move to Houston or someplace, and we'll see each other once a year, plus Instagram." He could see she was crying. "I'm sorry, Mom. I didn't mean it. I'll try to like him."

She hugged him.

Chapter Nine: Christmas, round two

Three days before he was to head back to school, his cell phone rang. "Lewis. Hey, hi. What ya doing?"

"I got a friend going back to school in Toledo, says he'll drop me off at your place, if you can get me back to school with you."

"Sure, Lew. That'd be fun. I'll ask Mom." He walked into the living room and told his mom the story.

"Lewis? Your roommate? Sure, he's welcome here for a couple days. Of course I'll take you both back to school."

"You hear that, Lew? You're in. When you coming?"

"As soon as I can get there. It's noon. Uh, it takes like two hours to get there, maybe longer with this flurry stuff going on. Gotta pack… Four o'clock?"

"That's great. I'll tell Mom. See you."

"He's going to be here at four, Mom. I'll do the laundry and set up his room."

"It will be nice to see your roommate again, Ted. I love it so much when he comes. He's really easy -- an easy guest."

"He eats a lot, remember. Do you think we have enough food to make it 'til Friday morning?"

"Don't worry. I'll handle Lewis. You just get his room ready." *I would really like to handle Lewis a few times. Such a willing student, such a slow learner. He's fun.* "You're right, though. I'm going to go get some groceries. Want anything special?"

"Nothing special for Lewis, Mom. Just a *lot* of whatever you get."

* * *

Jill got into the car, pulled out of the drive, and pulled out her phone. "Hi, Sherry?" They talked about their sons for the ten minutes it took to get to the store, Jill stocking up on things Lewis liked.

On her way home, Jill called Sherry again. "All set. Thanks, Sherry. Hey, do you ever tell Lewis how much we talk – you and I?"

"No. He thinks we're just intuitive, how things work out. You tell Ted?"

"No. There's no need for him to know. Let's just keep letting then think we're psychic."

"Jill, you're a rat. A good mom, and a ton of fun. But you're a rat." Sherry was laughing.

"And you're enabling me," Jill said. "Thanks for that."

"We've got to meet some time, Jill."

"And spoil our image? Well, it would be fun. Just, let's make sure we keep talking, keep the boys guessing."

"We're both rats," Sherry said. "But we love our sons. Happy New Year."

"You, too, rat-girl," and they hung up as Jill approached her subdivision.

* * *

Lewis had just arrived at Ted's. "Hi, Lew. Mom's still shopping. Your room's all ready. Happy New Year."

"Same to you, Ted. Thanks. Say, speaking of New Year's, what's up with that? What are we going to do?"

"Hadn't thought of that, actually. We can get on line, see what's going on."

"Well, we've got a day to figure that out. So, how was Christmas?"

"Pretty good, mostly. I got a few surprises. You?"

"Sherry's got a boyfriend. Basically just like my dad was, except he drinks more and hits less."

"Less?"

"Zero. I told him if I ever heard that he hit Sherry, I'd kill him." He chuckled. "He believed me, mellowed right out."

"So he's a drunk, not a brute?"

"More or less. More drunk. No brute. Sloppy drunk. Not dangerous, just repulsive. But I still don't want him around Sherry."

"She's a grownup."

"Yeah, but she's the only 'mom' I'll ever have."

"You never call her 'Mom.'"

"Her choice."

"Would you kill him, really?"

"I don't know. More to the point, neither does he."

Jill walked in. "Who wants a dinner of Dutch Apple pie à la mode?"

"Hi, Mom. I'll get the rest of the groceries. Lewis is here."

"Hello, Miss Jill. I'll help Ted with the groceries."

"Thank you, Lewis."

They were soon enjoying a New Year's Eve "dinner" of Blackbird's pie and Munchie's take-out vanilla with some kind of stuff in it that made it even sweeter and therefore better.

"This is incredible, Miss Jill," Lewis said. "You have to have the best food in Ohio."

"We try to eat healthy, Lewis," she said. "This isn't normal. But it's a special celebration. Are you ready to go back to work next week?"

"Mom, don't spoil it." And they all laughed.

"We'll have healthy meals from now on, provided," she looked at them sternly, "provided you finish every bit of this pie and ice cream tonight."

"No problem, Miss Jill. Thanks for watching out for our health. We'll do our part… Hey Ted, is there any more ice cream?"

As soon as the boys had showered and gone to bed, Jill did the same.

At one in the morning, she walked into Lewis's room, wearing her robe, the sash loose and the front open. He awoke, startled when he felt her finger against his lips.

She sat on the floor and then lay down, her robe open, her arms still in. Lewis pulled off his shorts and rolled silently atop her. "Let's see if you remember anything," she said, and this time, he started slowly, rubbing all over her body, taking his time.

Whether Nicole had made a difference or he was disoriented from having been asleep thirty seconds earlier didn't matter. It worked. Jill moaned, and Lewis put the tip of his finger lightly on her lips.

She opened her mouth and sucked his finger in. Then she took his wrists and spread them apart above her head, bringing his lips in contact with hers. He straightened out from his kneeling position and laid down on top of her, both of them wanting to breathe, both needing to stay silent.

She released his hands and ran hers down between their bodies, guiding him into her. "Now don't move," she said, as he laid his weight on her, his upper body resting on his elbows.

She moved a little, side to side. He moved with her. "No, you go the other way," she said. *He still has a lot to learn, but he's calmer, at least.* "Easy, slow. Follow my movement, but opposite. That's it. Keep the pressure on. More. More, Lewis. No, more."

She started to quiver a bit, then shake, and Lewis was getting alarmed. He started to get up, but she grabbed around behind his butt and pulled him deep into her, then clamped shut on him, unbelievably tight.

He came, and he kept coming, as she writhed and twisted below him, biting at his tongue and alternately grabbing the back of his head and then his butt, twisting, pulling, and all in total silence.

And she collapsed, stopped moving, looked into his eyes, and smiled. "Good night, Lewis," in the softest whisper. And she was gone.

It was like that, better each time, on nine more occasions before the trip back to school two days later.

She was making breakfast. The car was loaded. "Miss Jill, I don't know how you have to time or the energy to do all that you do," Lewis said.

"You say, 'for my age,' and you're going to starve."

"No, I mean, I get tired just trying to keep up." Ted looked at him. "I mean, just keeping your schedule, and you're doing all the work, besides."

"Eat your oatmeal, then check your rooms and the bath. Make sure you're not forgetting to pack something."

Lewis left the table first. Ted stayed behind. "Mom, you're the greatest." He started doing the dishes. "What Lew said, about your incredible energy, everything you do for us. It's amazing. I'm used to the dorm, but I think I'm going to miss you more than ever this term."

She looked into his eyes and he said, "For one thing, this term is longer." He gave her a little kid look, faked.

"Oh, stop it. Is all your stuff in the car? Got everything?"

"Yes, Mom. I loaded before breakfast."

"And I'm all set, too," Lewis said. "Just this backpack. Everything's in it. Thanks again, Miss Jill."

The only one not sleeping on the trip to Columbus was Jill. "Well, here we are again. Just like before, but you're so much more experienced now," she said, waking them up in the parking lot nearest their dorm. "Study hard. Be good."

"Thanks, Mom."

"Thanks a whole lot, Miss Jill."

"It was nice having you."

"It was nice being had." They laughed and walked away, back to the dorm.

"It's okay. I'm just… protective."

"Don't worry 'bout it. Sorry, even."

"We're good."

The room looked just as they had left it, but it smelled dead.

"What the hell did that mean, 'It was nice being had'?"

"Just an expression, man. I say it all the time. It's a reflex. Chill, all right?"

Chapter Ten: The seed of the crime

Routine reasserted itself, but this semester was missing a few of the fun students. There weren't as many parties. The dorm was quieter. And the schoolwork, as promised, was tougher, as was the competition. The un-serious students weren't back, and they included Nicole, who hadn't said a word to Lewis since that night he left forty bucks on her bed. Convenient as she was, he wanted a change.

It was their first day back. "What would you say, Ted, if we took down the bunk bed and set up the room like everybody else's?"

"Why?"

"I feel like I live in a cave, and this being dark all the time isn't helping."

"I hate it, too. I'm so close to the ceiling, it's hard to turn over. And I keep thinking I'm going to fall off this thing one night or another."

"Why didn't you say something?"

"Why didn't you?"

They moved enough stuff around that the top bed had a place to sit. The plastic milk crates slid under, just right. "I'm going to flip my mattress," Ted said. "That's supposed to be good for it."

"It is," Lewis confirmed, as he picked his up by the edge… and a handgun fell to the floor. "Ummm… I was going to tell you about that, Ted."

"Well, start talking. You could get expelled."

"We could get arrested, and expelled."

"*We?*"

"Yes, we. Even if I told them you didn't know anything about it, would they believe me? No. They find this, we're both screwed."

"So what the hell are you doing with it?"

"It's my dad's. I mean, it was. It's special to me. It was his backup. It was special to him. He loaded his own bullets for it and everything."

"Great. It's special to me, too. *The gun that got me a felony record, wrecked my career before it began, and started me on a life of crime.* Very cool, Lewis *effing* Foreman. I don't want to see it again, and as far as I'm concerned, I never saw it this time either."

"Thanks, man. Thanks, really. I didn't want to bring it, but I didn't want to leave it at home, where Sherry or that bum might find it."

"Did Sherry know where it was?"

"Probably. I don't know. I mean, why wouldn't she?"

"Won't she know it's gone?"

"I don't think she goes in the attic very much. Last few years, she's always sent me up there to get stuff or put things away. Christmas decorations, some screens for the windows…"

"What if she goes looking for it?"

"She won't know when it disappeared. She might think she just put it somewhere else, or she might think the cops that investigated my dad's murder might have found it and taken it with them, not said anything. But I don't think she'd ever look for it. And like I said, she might not even know where it was, in the first place. I'm sure not going to ask her."

"You didn't really bring it here to protect her, did you?"

Lewis hung his head. "No. I found it while I was getting the decorations. It was just kind of up there, half buried in insulation. I found it because I accidentally got my hand into the pink stuff. And there it was. I guess I just wanted it. It was my dad's. It should be mine."

"Is it loaded?"

Lewis looked into the cylinder, pointing the gun at his own face.

"*Jeezus*, Lewis!"

"Yes, it's loaded."

"Well, put it where I'll never find it. I didn't see it, remember. And think of some place to stash it until the next time you go home."

"Thanks for being cool about it, Ted. I owe you one."

"Just get it gone… Hell. Let's put the room back together. Hell."

* * *

"Lewis, you asleep?"

"Huh? No, shithead. I'm listening to you. What? What time is it?"

"Three-fifteen. I was just thinking about something."

"What?"

"Why do you think they never caught the guy who killed your dad?"

"You just won't let it go, will you? God, you're more interested in my dad's murder than either Sherry or I am. What's with you?"

"I'm just really curious, and, well, completely not about this being your dad – think how cool it would be to solve a murder. They dropped the investigation awfully quick. There's got to be more to it, maybe a dirty cop, or a gang from the prison, that works inside and outside…"

"Just, let it be, okay? Shit! I *told* you. I don't think they liked him, either. He was probably an asshole to them, too. Maybe they knew he beat up Sherry. Maybe one of them did it. Maybe somebody important got murdered, and they forgot about my dad. Hell, I don't know." He let a moment pass.

Ted, having released a demon in his roommate, breathed shallow, but his heart was so loud Lewis probably heard it.

Lewis spoke, calmer. "So since you won't drop this, what are you thinking?"

"I'm thinking maybe, since the file is old, they'd let you see it, and we could do some forensic work this summer and catch the guy who did it. That'd be cool, wouldn't it?"

"Like I said, I don't really care who did it. I'm just glad somebody did."

"But don't you want to know? Don't you want to know why they stopped looking? Maybe they're just missing a clue, somebody who saw it, or heard it happen."

"I *told* you, they didn't have enough clues." Then, calmer, "That's what they said, anyway."

"Maybe they didn't have enough clues because they didn't want to see them, or else they just overlooked something simple."

"Like what?"

"Like… I don't know. But from what you said, they hit a dead end real quick, and that was that. Doesn't that seem weird to you? Did they ask you anything?"

"I told them I was asleep. I didn't know anything."

"Were you?"

"Yes, as a matter of fact, I was. I sorta heard some firecrackers, I told them. I didn't know those were the shots. Then I fell asleep again, until the sirens."

"What else did they ask you?"

"Nothing. I went back to bed. Sherry told me what happened in the morning. I didn't even know Dad was dead until breakfast."

"Oh, god. That sucks. Did they ever ask you anything again?"

"No. I told them everything I knew, which wasn't much."

"Did they find the murder weapon, any clues?"

"I don't think so. Like I said, I haven't thought about it much. Really, I'm just relieved. Curious, maybe a little. I'd like to shake his hand."

"Whose? The guy who shot your dad?"

"Yeah."

"Lew, that's sick."

"You didn't know him. Can I go back to sleep now, or you got more curiosity running in your brain?"

"Yeah. Thanks. G'night."

Lewis dozed off in ten seconds, but Ted lay awake, thinking for an hour. He didn't know when he fell asleep, but the alarm seemed early.

Chapter Eleven: Bit by Jessica

"Hi, Jessica. So, you made it through okay? Are those new leggings?" Jessica had nice legs. Her sweater was snug and didn't go too far past her waist. She had a different look today, overall. Something…

"Yes, Ted. Got an A, same as you. Ninety-seven on the final."

"Ninety-five here. Hey, I'm glad you're back. Did you get the courses we talked about?"

"All of them. We have, like, three of the same classes together, plus lab."

They saw a lot of each other in class, then a lot more, studying. It happened after lab, on a Wednesday, late afternoon.

"Jess, that lab was brutal. Chemistry I like, but now he's throwing physics in, and calculus."

"There's math in everything, Ted. We don't have to like it, but it's, well, it's, …we gotta do it, so…"

"You're right. You're always right. But it's okay to hate it just a little, isn't it?"

"Hate it all you like. Just do it."

* * *

Jessica wasn't an easy lab partner, but she was good, keeping Ted focused. Not telling him things he had to know, but telling him how he had to go learn them. And Jessica was like his mom in that way – always in charge, and always looking out for him at the same time. And Ted was smart. He never doubted her motives or her conclusions. And he always took her advice.

Jessica liked that. Her innate fear of men never took a foothold when she was with the unassuming, quiet, trusting, honest, naïve Ted. He was easy to be with, if not exciting.

So she was surprised that day, when Ted said, "Jessica?" She looked, stopped walking. "I've been thinking, and I think I like you a lot more than just a lab partner." She didn't say a thing. "I'd like to…"

She slowly put her books down, right near the door. It was cold, but not near as cold as ten feet farther, where the snow had stopped falling, but the wind was still fighting to hold the door open. Right there, she grabbed the collar of his jacket and pulled his face cown to hers, and kissed him, hard.

"You're cutting this afternoon," she said. She was right, again.

* * *

It was inevitable, beautiful, clumsy, and self-conscious. After all, they were both virgins, and it's not like in the books or movies. Which they hadn't watched many of, regardless.

* * *

Ted didn't tell Lewis right away, but Lewis noticed a change in his roommate. "Hey, Ted, how's Jessica? Still studying hard together? Still hard studying together?"

"Shut up, Lew. It's easy studying together. And it's not hard all the time any more, either." Lew caught the smirk on Ted's face.

"You mean…? Ted smiled. "You and Jessica? You rotten bastard -- when were you going to tell me?"

"When it became your business, which it isn't. But… yes. I love her, Lewis."

"Oh, here you go. Pussy-whipped already, by a freshman virgin, no less. She's a virgin, right?"

"Well, uhhh, she was. But shut up, Lew. Not a word to anybody. As far as anybody knows, we're study buddies, that's all. And that goes especially for my mom."

"Ted's got a girlfriend. Ted's got a girlfriend!"

"Shup up, Lew," and he threw his shoes at him as Lewis hopped around the room like an idiot, making fun of a guy he was envying with all his heart.

Chapter Twelve: Exchange students

The snow, such as there was that winter, was gone, and thoughts were on Spring Break.

"Ted, what are you doing for break?"

"Going home, studying, helping Mom around the place. There's always something needs fixed or cleaned up. You?"

"Probably the same. Sherry's already said there's a few things she needs help with. You know how to do anything?"

"Like what? Handyman things? I'm okay with plumbing, simple stuff. I worked last summer with some roofers. Mostly grunt work, carrying bundles of shingles up ladders, but yeah, I guess I learned a couple things. What're you thinking?"

"I'm thinking, you've never seen my house, met Sherry. And I already know she's got a list for me. Suppose you come to my place for a few days?"

"Well, maybe, but Mom's got stuff for me to do, too. I guess. I'll ask."

"Okay, let's make it better. You come help me at my place for a couple days, help Sherry. Then we go to your place and help your mom."

"You make break sound like so much fun."

"Would you rather do your own place for the whole week, without help, or get it done faster, with my help? And do the same thing in Chillicothe?"

"Lew, I've never even been to Chillicothe."

"All the more reason you ought to visit. See the world."

"The world? Chillicothe?"

"You'll never know unless you check it out. Why not? We'll still get stuff done, and we'll get it done quicker if we help each other. And besides, while you're there, we can go to the police and see my dad's file."

"For real? Now, that would be fun. Cool. I'll ask Mom."

* * *

"Spring Break starts Friday, Ted. What're we going to do?"

"I'll call Mom today, promise. Did you talk to Sherry? And did you call the police, see if they'll let us look at the files?"

"Sherry said yes. I told you two days ago. I didn't call the police."

"When I was studying for a chem test with Jess, right. I don't remember a thing. Okay, let's call my mom."

"Hi, Mom. Hey, Lewis and I just had this idea for break. We visit each other's houses, help each other with whatever needs fixing. Take a couple days, each place. Could we do that?"

"Ahh, sure. I don't really have a list of things to do, but I'm sure I could use some help with things. When…?"

"We'd go to his house in Chillicothe for the Friday, Saturday, Sunday, Monday, then come up to Mansfield."

"Oh, honey, that's not good. I'd really like you home soon as possible. Could you boys come here first?"

Ted turned to Lewis, explained. "That would give us more time at my place."

Lewis said, "Weekdays – we could see the police. I'll tell Sherry. It'll be okay. Say yes."

"Sure, Mom. That's even better. How are we going to get out of here, though? Will you come pick us up?"

"I can pick you up on Friday. Actually, you can have the car to go down to Lewis's house. Jack's staying here all week, and we can use his SUV. Then come back here, bring Lewis if you want, for the last day or so, and I'll drive you both back to Columbus."

Jack? That pervert's still around? "Yeah, uh… okay, Mom. Uh, where will we all be sleeping?"

"I'll have that all worked out. Don't worry about it. I'll see you Friday. Love you!"

They hung up. Ted turned to Lewis, green in the face. "What's up, bro?"

Ted said, "Mom's boyfriend, Jack. He's going to be there all week. We at least get to use Mom's car to go to Chillicothe, Sunday afternoon. We'll bring it back after we're caught up at your place, drive back to Mansfield, stay there probably for theweekend. Then Mom's going to drive us back here."

"And when will this guy, Jack, be there?"

"Starting at least Sunday, until we bring her car back. I don't know. She said not to worry about where we all sleep."

"Well, what the hell, right? We'll get everything done, you'll meet Sherry. I'll meet Jack. It'll be like family reunion week."

"Except for Jack. I can't stand him, and I don't like him with my mom."

"I don't even know him, and I hate him, too. So, let's get our stuff together. Your mom's going to be here in two days. I've got laundry to do."

* * *

"Hi, Mom," Ted said as he and Lewis tossed their backpacks in the trunk of the Taurus.

"Hi, Ted. You look great. And Lewis, I'm so glad you're coming again."

"Me. Too, Miss Jill. Thanks for having me."

On the way to Mansfield, Ted asked, "So what are the room arrangements, Mom? You said Jack's going to be there, too?"

"Oh, we worked it out. It's perfect, really. He's going to get to our house on Sunday, for lunch. Then after lunch, I understand you'll be heading to Lewis's house. Chillicothe, right?"

"Right," Lewis said.

"So you can have the car to go to Lewis's for the whole week. Just be back home no later than Friday afternoon. Jack has to be back in Dayton on Saturday morning. He's leaving Friday."

"So Lewis and I get our rooms?"

"Yes. I'll just change the bedding when you leave, then on Friday again."

"You don't have to do both rooms, Mom. Just the guest room."

"You're always thinking of ways to save me trouble, Ted. I love that about you."

"So it will be like old times?" Lewis was asking several questions, and Jill answered them all.

"Yes, Lewis," Jill said. "Exactly like old times, both weekends."

"That'll be fun."

"I'm – we're all – counting on it," she said. And the rest of the way, they sat in silence, Jill driving, Lewis checking his phone in the back seat, Ted up front, sleeping.

* * *

"Okay, everybody out. Same rooms as usual. Get your stuff organized, then come to the kitchen for some food," Jill said.

Lewis went to the end of the hall, tossed his backpack on the bed and came right back out, brought the spare chair into the kitchen, and sat in his usual place at the round table. "Oh, sorry, Miss Jill," he said. "Is there anything I can do to help?"

"Set three places, if you would. Silverware's in the left-hand drawer. Napkins are in the pantry over there, top shelf."

Ted walked into the kitchen and saw Lewis setting places. "What can I do?"

"Waters, please," his mom said, "and ice all around."

* * *

That night, and again on Saturday morning when Ted was mowing the lawn for the first time in the new year, and again three times on Saturday night, Jill and Lewis had sex. Always quiet, on the floor, in the guest room. Except when Ted was mowing the lawn, it was on Lewis's bed, as they listened with one ear to the lawn mower go by the window, shades drawn.

When Jack arrived at noon on Sunday, Lewis was still thinking about that time on the bed.

"Hi, I'm Jack Pope," he said. "I was expecting Ted. Who might you be?"

"I'm Ted's roommate, Lewis. I'm, we're heading down to my place right after lunch, coming back Friday afternoon. She – Miss Jill – said you had something early morning on Saturday in – where was that? – Dayton?"

"Yes, we have a meeting at the Air Force Museum. I'm on the board there. They're building a new exhibit hangar. Too many airplanes."

"They have meetings on Saturday mornings?"

"It's a good time to get everybody together when they can't pretend they have other business," Jack said.

"Well, hi. Nice to meet you, Mister Pope."

"Jack."

"Jack." Then Lewis went to Ted's room. "He's here. Let's get packing."

"Yeah, I don't want to see him any more than I have to. I'm ready now. When can you get packed?"

"As soon as I unplug my computer. Give me five minutes, clean my stuff out of the bathroom. You want me to strip the bed?"

"Good idea," Ted said, and they both laughed. For different reasons.

"Thanks, Mom," Ted said, as he and Lewis headed for the door. "See you Friday."

"Yes, thank you, Miss Jill. I hope we earned our keep this weekend."

"Oh, you did, Lewis, you did. But why," she looked at both of them, "are you leaving so fast? I made lunch. Aren't you boys hungry?"

"Mom, we promised Sherry we'd get some things done today, even. Really, we'll be fine." Then, "Nice to see you again, Jack." And he and Lewis headed for the Taurus.

"Think she noticed?" Ted asked.

"You mean, that we're out of there like a couple Polaris missiles from a submarine? Yes, I think she noticed. I don't think Jack cared, though." Then, "She's serious about him? God, he's so old. And fat."

"Mom's looking out for her future," Ted said. "She told me that. 'There's a lot more to life than just how people look,' she said. 'How they make you feel, how they treat you. How secure they make you feel,' she told me."

"He's got money," she means.

"Well, that's part of it, I guess. I don't think she's in it for his looks."

"I'll say," Lewis said. "He's this big ball of butter, and he's old. And your mom, she's so…"

"Drop it, Lew," Ted said. And he did.

* * *

"Say, Ted, mind if I ask you something?"

Ted looked over at Lewis. "It's a long way to Chillicothe. Just don't let me miss any turns."

"Did you see Jack's car? The black Buick SUV?"

"Yeah."

"I think that's the one I saw when I walked your mom to the parking lot, back when we met at orientation."

"I sorta wondered that back at Christmas, but I forgot about it. You sure?"

"It's identical, if it isn't the one. Even that stupid CB antenna. How many of those do you think there are in this part of Ohio?"

"Yeah, or the world."

"You're doing fine for the next twenty miles. Keep going straight. Another question?" Ted nodded. "What I wanted to ask you, you seem to really hate Jack. What's that about?"

"You don't like him, either. Why's that?"

"I don't like him," Lewis said. "He's slimy. I just don't like him. But you, you really seem to hate the guy. Did he do something to your mother? Did your watch stop?"

"Shut up, Lew. No, as far as she tells me, he's a perfect gentleman. Whatever that means, and I don't want to know. But last Christmas when he was at our house -- didn't I tell you about that?"

"No, you just came back and you didn't like him. You didn't say why, and I didn't ask. None of my business, unless you tell me. But something's definitely bothering you."

So Ted told Lewis about the hand on his leg, how there could be no mistake, no accident.

"The guy's your mom's boyfriend, and he's hitting on you, too?" Lewis was not confused. He was angry, that temper he had told Ted about, but that Ted had never actually seen. It seemed an over-reaction. Even scared Ted a little.

"Look, Lew, it's none of my business to tell Mom. He's her boyfriend, and he didn't try anything today."

"It is your business. And he 'didn't try anything,' when, for the three minutes we were all together in the house? Your mom needs to know."

"I'll tell her when the time is right."　　"What, you're just going to wait until she's wearing his big diamond ring and then say, 'Oh by the way, Mom, Jack's a pervert, and he's gay for me?' Man, you've got to tell her."

"I will. I swear. I'm just going to do it when it's the right time."

"Here's some advice from a guy who's seen a lot of relationships come and go: don't wait, Ted. It won't get better if you don't tell her."

"Maybe they'll break up anyway."

"Yeah. Maybe hell freezes this year. Climate change and all that." They sat silent for a while. "You just keep driving. You've got another two, three miles. This road comes to a T intersection. Take a left there."

Chapter Thirteen: Sleuthin'

Ted steered the Taurus up the two track gravel drive with fresh green weeds growing in the middle, and stopped in the carport. They got their backpacks and headed to the house.

"Hi, Lewis. Welcome home. Happy Easter." Sherry was smiling in the doorway. "And Ted? So nice to meet you."

"Nice to meet you, too, Missus Foreman." As soon as he said that, he remembered, but it was too late.

"Hobart. Just call me Sherry. Everybody calls me Sherry."

"Sure, okay. Thank you, Sherry. It's nice to finally meet you. Lew's been trying to get me here since August."

"You've never been to Chillicothe?" she asked.

"Never had a reason, I guess, or an opportunity, 'til I met Lewis. Thanks, Sherry. I'm glad to be here."

"Lewis, show Ted the room. I'm just thrilled you're both here."

They entered through the living room. Lewis dropped his backpack on the sofa, then turned right and pointed down the short hallway. "Your room's at the end of the hall. There's the bathroos on the right. Sherry's the bedroom on the left."

"Where are you?"

"Right here," he said. "The couch pulls out. It's one of those things turns into a bed. It's really comfortable."

"Fouton?"

"Yeah, that. See?" He pulled it out. It looked comfy. "I've got a spare set of sheets and stuff right here," and he opened the stereo cabinet, bottom right door. "We do this whenever there's a guest. It's fine."

"Well, thanks, Lew, but I'd rather you use your own room."

"No, this is our family, our house," he grinned, "and our rules. I sleep here. Deal or no deal?"

"Like you said, it's your house. Thanks." And Ted went to his room, really Lewis's room, and put his backpack on the floor. He kicked off his shoes and laid down on the twin bed with a sag in the middle. *Like a hammock, but it doesn't swing. More like a nest. No wonder he likes the couch. Quit griping, Ted, you snob.*

After a quick lunch and after Ted helped his roommate clear some dead tree limbs off the fence in the back yard, Sherry suggested Lewis show Ted around town.

Ted drove, Lewis navigated the sights of Chillicothe. "We don't have a prison museum like you do in Mansfield," Lewis said. "We have the real deal, like your new prison. It's where my dad worked."

"Must be tough, knowing somebody killed him, never got punished for it."

"Like I said, I'd like to shake his hand. But yeah, I wonder about the quality or even the sincerity of our police, when a guy, practically a cop himself, at least a member of law enforcement, a guy like that can get shot in front of his own house and nobody gets caught."

"Can we see the prison?"

"The outside, sure. We're almost there. Make a right."

"Nice looking place, but I wouldn't want to live there," Ted said, as they passed the forbidding fences and walls. "Probably not even visit. Prisons give me the creeps."

"Lots of bad people in there," Lewis said, "but hardly a one of them is guilty."

"What?"

"Just ask them. 'I was set up.' Or 'I wasn't the only one,' or 'They had to lock up somebody,' or one of Dad's favorites, 'Everybody else gets away with it, but I do it once, get caught, and I get thrown in here.'"

"So, they're in here, it's all somebody else's fault."

"Pretty much," Lewis said. "Something else that's weird about this city. See that cemetery?"

"What about it?"

"Well, that's the city's cemetery, but nobody living in the city is allowed to be buried in it."

"That's crazy. Why?"

"Because if they're *living* in the city, nobody's allowed to bury them anywhere."

"Lewis, that's just bad. But it's funny."

"Hey, Ted. Change the subject. Remember I told you Sherry's sort of seeing a guy?"

"Uhhh… maybe?"

"Well, she isn't. So don't mention it, okay?"

"Sure, okay. It's getting dark. Which way is home?"

Lewis pointed.

* * *

They were home in ten minutes, hungry.

"Ted, do you like burgers?"

"Yes, absolutely." Dinner: fried hamburgers, baked sweet potatoes, and green peas, was followed by Fudgesicles.

"Thank you, Sherry. Great dinner," Ted said, "and thanks for the Fudgesicles. I haven't had one of those in ages. I love 'em."

"One of Sherry's specialties," Lewis said. "Not the Fudgesicles, the great dinner. I don't know why I gained weight at school. The food here is so much better."

"That's the freshman fifteen," Sherry said. "Everybody seems to pack it on. I think it's from trying to make up for a lack of sleep by eating more. Do you boys get enough sleep?"

"Of course I do, Sherry. Stop worrying."

"You, Ted. Do you sleep enough?"

"Well, there's a lot going on at school. I think, really, we're always tired. If nobody woke me up, I'd sleep 'til Thursday. But I wouldn't want to miss a meal, either." He looked at Lewis. "Sooo conflicted!" They all laughed.

"What's on your schedule tomorrow?" Sherry asked.

"Whatever you need us to do around here," Lewis said. "Then,…"

"Then Lew and I want to go down to the police station and look at the cold case file on his dad," Ted said.

Sherry turned around from the counter where she was wrapping leftover sweet potatoes, looking serious. "My husband, Lewis's father, was murdered, right here, three years ago last winter. It's very painful for him to talk about it."

"I'm sorry, Missus Hobart. I didn't want…"

"Sherry, I saw how he treated you," Lewis said. "You saw how he treated me, too. I just don't think some killer should get away with killing."

"We don't expect to find anything, really," Ted offered, "but Lewis,… you heard what he said, and he wants closure. Me? I just think it would be an adventure, looking for a killer who's still on the loose in Chillicothe."

"Or not in Chillicothe," she said. "Or dead, or in prison for something else. These kinds of tigers don't change their spots."

She realized what she said, same time the boys did. The tension dissipated in laughter. "Oh, go for it. You never know what you'll find out. You may even turn out to be great detectives."

"Thanks, Sherry. It'll be interesting for me, but I'm really doing this for Lew."

* * *

"Here's what we have, Mister Foreman," said the desk sergeant, as he put a brown cardboard box on the table in what was usually an interrogation room. "This is everything. Well, not the photos, from the crime scene or the autopsy. Those are in another file, and I don't have access to that."

"Why are the crime scene photos not in the investigation folder?" Lewis said.

"I really don't know, son. That's unusual. The coroner has a separate filing system. The autopsy drawings are usually copied in the box I just gave you, but not the photos. The coroner will probably let you look at those whenever you want them, but the pictures won't tell you anything the sketches don't. And, I mean, he was your father. You might not want to see them, anyway."

"Maybe not. But we have plenty to look at here, anyway. Thanks."

"One last thing, real serious. Look at whatever you like. Make notes. If you need something copied, just holler. But nothing from this box leaves this room, understand?"

"Yes, sir. Thank you. Er, is there anyone here I could talk with about this, anyone who worked on it?"

"After you've read everything here, yeah. But read it all. You don't want to waste his time with questions that the answers are already in there."

"How late can we stay to look at this?"

"Until my shift is up – six o'clock. But you have to be out of here from noon to one. That's for lunch. And if we need the room for an interrogation, then right away, understood?"

"Yes, sir. Thank you, sir."

"Anything else?"

"No, I guess we'll get right into it. Thank you." And the sergeant left Lewis Foreman, Ted Hamlin, and the body – of evidence – of Garret Foreman alone at the table.

"What do you want to do?" Lewis said. "Should we go through this one folder at a time, so we don't get anything out of order, or just kind of look through the whole box and see if anything jumps out at us?"

"He said we should read everything before we talk to that detective. How about, you read from the front folder and I read from the back, work toward the middle? We tag anything, make notes about it, if it's particularly interesting."

"Works for me," Lewis said. "Here's yours." He handed a thin folder to Ted, pulled out a thicker one for himself. They sat down and started reading, making notes on separate papers, tearing off scraps to put into the folder, bookmarks for each other.

"So, we both read all of this," Ted said, "and look at each other's notes, and then we ask ourselves questions until we know what's here, and then we see if the detective will talk to us. That's the plan?"

"Sounds good to me. Need more paper, anything?"

"Nope. Let's get started."

Each started a timeline, noted basic facts. Not much talking, even when they went to lunch. Together, they summarized their findings:

```
No eyewitnesses, a couple people thought
they might have heard the shots. Sherry
heard the car door close, then she
thought she heard the shots, didn't know
how many. Three? Four? Fairly close
together, then a gap of a second or two,
then the last shot. Sherry found Garret
Foreman outside, by the front
door,called 911. Didn't see anybody or
hear anything. No car.
    Garret was dead at the scene, lying
face down, head toward the door, his
keys in his right hand. Three bullets
```

entered his chest. One was still in his
body. He had another bullet wound in the
back of his head, fired from above his
head, as if he were lying face down at
the shooter's feet when the *coup de
grace* was administered.

Only one bullet was recovered, the one
in his chest found during the autopsy. It
was a 115 grain full jacket "target"
bullet, typically fired from a three-
eighty, a "Makarov nine by eighteen," but
commonly from 'most any nine millimeter
semi-automatic handgun. Only one shell
casing was recovered, a nine, but it was
not definitively matched to that bullet or
to any identified handgun from any other
file. No weapon was recovered.

Interviews of neighbors didn't add
anything useful to Sherry's testimony.
Some heard three shots total; some four;
one heard five, some didn't know. Nobody
saw a car or a person, but no one
bothered to look outside. It was cold
and dark, and it was over quickly.

Police searched the immediate area,
but found no bullets other than the one
still in Foreman's body, and no shell
casings other than the one near the
front door, the 9mm that "could not be
positively identified as matching the
bullet in the victim's body."

"They never got past that?" Lewis said, after
each had been through the entire set of folders.
"Neighbors saw nobody. Sherry didn't see anybody.
They only found one bullet, one casing? There

were at least four of each – where are the other three, other four, maybe?"

"I think you're right," Ted said. "They didn't look very hard. No interviews of co-workers? No inquiry to see if any possible 'enemy' was missing from work, or had been seen around? Nothing at all on his bank records? Nothing?"

"Yeah, they really didn't put themselves out, did they?" Lewis put the last of the folders back in the box. It was five-thirty. "Let's see if that detective will talk to us tomorrow."

The desk sergeant said, "So, did you find what you were looking for?"

"Well, no, not really," Lewis said. "Do you think we could talk to that detective that worked on the case?"

"He's a patrolman."

"What happened to the detective?"

"The detective retired, moved to Arizona. But I'll see if I can catch our guy on the radio. He's off at six, too. Stand by." And they did.

"He can see you for half an hour before the start of his shift tomorrow, if you like. Seven-thirty. So you'd have him until eight. Would that work?" Lewis nodded. The sergeant said, "Yes, they'll be here, seven-thirty… Yeah, I know… Thanks, Joe."

"Be here seven-thirty sharp. Ask for Officer Leonard."

"Thank you, sergeant," Lewis said. "Good night." And they drove back to Sherry's, where chicken, rolls, and mashed potatoes, the Colonel's best, were in a big bucket on the table.

"Perfect timing, boys," Sherry said. "I just got home with this. Dig in." After the first round of extra-crispy had disappeared, she said, "So, did you two Sherlocks find out anything interesting?"

Lewis said, "Well, they didn't have much. You were the only decent witness, and you couldn't tell them a whole lot. But they really didn't look. I mean, they didn't even look at his banking, see if he was overdrawn or anything unusual, any pattern that didn't make sense. They basically asked you and some neighbors 'if you saw who did it,' and you didn't, so they went home."

"Lewis, I'm sure they did more than that. It seemed they were crawling all over the neighborhood for a week."

"Sherry," Ted said, "they only found one bullet. They only found one shell casing. But there were four bullet holes, four bullets, four shells. At least. And they only found one of each? And then, they couldn't be sure of a match between that casing and that bullet, for sure. Might have come out of a different gun, even. And no gun. They don't even know for sure what caliber it was – nine millimeter, a thing they call 'Makarov,' or three-eighty. All those are semi-automatics, so there should be four shell casings from four bullets. All they got was one of each, and they aren't sure the casing's even from that day, but probably."

"But," Lewis said, "the reports look like they didn't care at all. They didn't dig around. They didn't interview a single co-worker or his boss. They didn't look for anybody he owed money to."

He looked at Sherry. "Do you have his bank records from then? Anything – a checkbook, credit card records? We could go through those. Maybe there's a clue in there. God, Sherry, they didn't even look."

"Well, what do you do, now?" she asked.

"Tomorrow morning," Ted said, "we get to talk to one of the cops who remembers the case. Seven-thirty, for half an hour."

"A detective?"

"No, the detective's retired, moved to Arizona. This one's a patrolman. Not much, but at least he was on the case."

Lewis said, "Sherry, it might really help if we could see Dad's bank stuff. Do you know where it might be?"

"If it's here, it'll be in his desk, bottom right drawer. I haven't looked in there since…" Her voice drifted off. She started to sob.

"Oh, sorry, Sherry. I'm sorry. He was important to me, too, you know." And Lewis started to sob. Ted went to his room and turned out the light, sank into the pit in the middle of Lewis's mattress, and fell asleep.

It seemed only a minute had passed. Lewis shook him awake. "Ted, dessert, unless you want me to eat it all. Get up and wash your front feet."

A couple minutes later, Ted said, "Thanks, Sherry. This is good."

"Glad you like it. I slaved over a hot shopping cart, literally for minutes, picking out a cherry pie."

"Well, it's excellent. Thank you."

Then Lewis said, "Dad's bank stuff is right here." He pointed to a pile of paper and envelopes on the kitchen counter. "Want to have a look?"

"Why not?" Then Ted looked at Sherry. "You sure it's all right with you? I mean, it's kind of personal."

"Go for it, Ted," she said. "I can't see how it can hurt anything. I never paid attention to his finances. I mean, we paid the bills together. I never looked at his books, and when he died… when he died, they closed the account and moved the balances from our joint account and his personal account into my own. I have all that, too. You can see it. But I don't think there's anything interesting."

"Thanks, Sherry," said Lewis. "I'm really doing this, just to see if there's anything I can figure out about Dad's murder. I know you've always been perfect with the money. I just want you to know that I know that."

"I don't have any problem at all, Lewis. I mean, it's as good a time as any for you to learn about the finances of a household. I'm all for it."

Lewis turned to Ted. "Let's have at it." Ted nodded, and they walked to the kitchen counter and stood opposite each other, the bright ceiling light glaring down between them onto the papers. "I think Sherry's right," Lewis said, after an hour of looking at bank statements and checkbooks. "There's nothing unusual here, except for the three thousand dollars when Dad bought the boat, and the statement even says 'boat,' right there, like he was going to forget. Everything else is just boring."

Ted said, "Yeah, direct deposit from his job – I didn't know what guards made before… it's not very much, is it?" He looked at Lewis. Lewis was looking back. "No, I don't mean it that way. It's just, well, it explains maybe why our parents so badly want us to go to college."

"Anyway," Lewis said, "it's like Sherry said. He didn't make a lot of money and they didn't spend a lot of money, but there isn't anything that stands out. They marked everything – 'sofa' it says, or 'reloader,' or 'range hood.' Everything over about a hundred bucks on the credit cards is marked. Looks like they had a pretty solid relationship, at least when it came to money."

"It's really routine stuff," Ted said. "They saved a little, paid all their bills, and like you said, they didn't spend much. Model citizens, perfect customers at the bank."

"I don't think Dad was killed for money," Lewis said, half-laughing, half sad. "His life insurance…"

"Yes?"

"Just about every cent is going to Ohio State."

"I never thought about that," Ted said. "We never talk finances at our house. I got a scholarship – tuition – but room and board, books, fees, all that's got to be a lot. I don't know how Mom pays for it. My summer job – I give her half, but that can't be near enough."

* * *

They woke up tired and stayed that way en-route to the police station, but Lewis picked up the conversation. "Your mom works, right?"

"No, well, a little. She works for Richland County, in the tourism office sometimes, arranging events and stuff, you know, at the prison and the race track. It's part time, but she doesn't mind. And once in a while, like before Christmas, if she wants to, she works at the mall, one store or another. She did this year, last year, too. Most years she works before Christmas, but she says Dad's pension and insurance are enough for everyday."

Lewis let it sink in. "Don't ask."

"I won't. Rock the boat? Not me."

They rolled through the drive-up at McDonald's at seven-fifteen. The coffee hadn't yet kicked in when they met Patrolman Leonard a few minutes later.

"Good morning, gentlemen," he said.

"Hi, sir. Thanks for meeting with us," Lewis said. "I'm Lewis, this is Ted. Garret Foreman was my father."

"Well, how can I help?"

They went back to the interrogation room, where the box was on the table. Lewis and Ted pulled out their notes. Lewis began.

"I'm not wanting to sound like a smart ass or anything, sir, but Ted and I have looked all through this case file, and well, there's nothing here. You – and I mean all the police, not 'you,' personally – you asked Sherry what she saw and heard, asked a few neighbors, and found a shell casing. There's no mention of you guys' interviewing anybody else. Nobody from work, no relatives, nobody from his bank… nobody. It just seems that, and this is just me – I know you're busy – it seems that nobody was all that interested in finding out who killed my dad."

"Now Lewis," Leonard said, "there weren't any clues, and we did ask your mom if she heard or saw…"

"Sherry's not my mom." Edgy, because the cop at the scene should have known that.

"Oh, sorry, Lewis. I knew that. Sorry, okay?" Lewis nodded. "We asked everybody in the neighborhood, and nobody knew anything at all.

There weren't any tire tracks or footprints. You saw that in the report, right?" Again, a nod. "No footprints, no prints on the one shell casing we found, no gun, nobody mad at him, no debts, -- I mean, look at it. There's just no clues. We simply had nothing to go on. The case is still open. If anything turns up…"

Ted said, "If I may?" Leonard looked straight at him. "We were wondering where the other bullets and shells might be, and why they couldn't be found. One bullet was recovered from the body. Maybe the other two in his chest just kept on going, you can't find them. But the one fired from above him, the one through his head…" Lewis clenched his jaw, but nodded for Ted to go on. "That one – where could it be? It has to be right below Mister Foreman's face. Why couldn't they find it?"

"I really don't have a good answer for that, uh… Ted. I was new on the force, and I wasn't there for the on-site investigation, or even for the interviews. I mostly just wrote those reports you have there, from what I was told."

"Does it make sense to you that they couldn't find that bullet, and only one shell? I mean, how far can the shells have gone?"

"Maybe he – the murderer – maybe he picked them up."

"He seemed to be gone pretty fast, and he's going to hang around, looking for brass in the dark? And the bullet? If it wasn't in the body and nobody found it, it should still be there, right on the sidewalk or just under a paver, shouldn't it?"

"Well, it's been almost four years…"

"Yeah, but where else would it be?"

Lewis said, "If we went back to my house, suppose we found the bullet. Would that help? We could look around for shells, too."

"After all this time, there's no way we could tell if whatever you might find would be related to your father's murder," Leonard said.

"But if the bullet matched the one in the autopsy and the shell matched the one you already found…"

Leonard smiled. "It couldn't hurt."

Lewis looked over at Ted. "Let's go snoop around my house."

"Good luck, son."

"Thanks, Officer Leonard."

On the way home, Ted said, "Strange."

"What's strange?"

"Strange that we don't even know exactly where your dad's body was placed. No pictures of the scene at all."

"We forgot to ask. Crap. But Sherry will remember, I'll bet you anything."

"Pictures would be precise. Sherry must've been pretty shook up."

"Well, damn it, Ted, we'll ask her, okay?"

"Don't bite me. I'm trying to help."

"Sorry, man."

* * *

Sherry was just getting up, fixing her own breakfast, when Lewis and Ted came in. "Sherry," Lewis said, "can you show us exactly – exactly where Dad was, when you found him?"

She looked up, hesitated for effect. "Well, good morning, Lewis. Good morning, Ted. Did you find out anything useful at the police?"

"Sorry, Sherry," Lewis said. "It's just – they did such a slacker job, we thought maybe we could find more shells, maybe even a bullet, if we knew where to start looking."

"How could I forget? Go do something for a few minutes, while I have my breakfast. Then I'll show you exactly how I remember things."

Lewis was doing the dishes as Sherry ate, and he took her plate and coffee cup as soon as they were emptied. "Okay, okay," Sherry said. "Let's go outside."

"Here is where I found Garret. Right here. Two pavers from the steps. I remember counting." She shook her head and threw her hands up in the air. "I have absolutely no idea why I paid attention to that, or how I remembered it. Your mind just does crazy things when you're under stress. This," and she bent down and outlined with her hands "is where his head was. He stretched out that way,"
she pointed "from here. I remember he was pretty straight, like he was standing up, but he was lying down. I thought that looked strange."

"Two pavers, and then his head on the third one?" Ted asked.

"Right, and straight out, that direction. Can I go back in, now?" Sherry was in tears.

"Sure," Lewis said. "Thanks so much. Sorry to ask you. We'll take it from here." She went inside, and then to Ted, "That's helpful. Let's think a minute. If he's here, coming toward the house, and he's shot in the chest… the shell would eject to the right, so it should be over there somewhere," as he gestured at the bushes. "And the shot, the one in his head, that would have been fired from like, from the first or second paver. Maybe the shooter didn't move. Just stood here in front of the house. But why would he just stand there and get shot at point-blank range?"

"Hey," Ted said, "you know what we didn't ask? We didn't ask where the shell was found. Was it from there," he nodded to the yard "or there, in the bushes?"

"And why wasn't that mentioned in the report, anyway? Who are these Keystone Kops?"

"Lewis, I hate to say it, but your PD sucks."

"Worse than I thought. Well, let's start looking. I'll go inside, get a spoon."

"For?"

"For to dig up the bullet that went through my father's head. If Sherry's remembering, we're just about standing on it. Why don't you start in the bushes, look for the shells?"

Lewis picked up the third paver and started scratching the dirt, beginning at the edge of the second one. Ted was in the bushes near the front door for no more than two minutes when he said, "Lewis! Look at this – I think I found one."

"Don't move. Keep your eye on it," and Lewis readied his smart phone and took a distant shot, then one of just the bush, then a closeup of the shell. It was stuck at the bottom of the center of the bush in a tiny pile of dead leaves and broken sticks, just your typical bunch of dead natural stuff at the base of a bush. "Don't touch it. I'll go get a plastic bag."

"Sherry – Ted found a shell casing in the bush," as he ran to the kitchen to get a plastic bag.

"Is it from…"

"I don't know, but it's a shell casing, and it's five feet from our front door. That sounds pretty good to me." And he ran back outside. "Ted, get a little stick to pick it up. I don't want our prints on it, and I don't want to wreck one, if it's on there."

"Wow," Ted said. "I sure didn't think we'd find one so fast. I really didn't think we'd find one at all, if you want to know the truth."

"Neither did I. Cool, Ted. Really cool. I'm just going to lay this baggie over here, by the porch. Now I gotta find that bullet."

Another hour of looking and scratching yielded nothing. Sherry came outside with a pitcher of iced tea. "Sherlock, Watson, y'all want some tea?"

"Sherry, we're right here," Lewis said. "You don't have to shout like we're halfway across town."

"I'm just excited, Lewis. And I'm a little disappointed you didn't include me in this."

"I'm sorry, but you were crying. And I don't know why we – you and I – never thought to do this on our own."

"I don't know. I guess I just didn't want to get in the way of the police, you know, disturb evidence or something."

"It's okay. It is. And I never thought of it, either. I mean, if the police gave up, they must have had their reasons. At least I thought so.

Sherry looked startled. "What do you think, now?"

"I don't know. I mean, either we have the worst police force in the universe – I mean, look. Ted found a shell casing in just a couple minutes. So either they are stupid, or…"

"Or what?"

"Sherry, I don't want to think it."

"Or what, Lewis?"

"Or they know who killed Dad, and they don't want him caught. I mean, that detective moved to Arizona right after."

"He retired, and it was more than a year after, remember? You told me."

"There's just something wrong. Something… I don't know what. But we'll find it, right, Ted?"

Ted had been between the bush and the house, not moving. "But we will find something. You want another shell casing?"

"You're kidding, right? I mean, you found another one?"

"Right here. I was scraping the old leaves and stuff from along the wall, and, well, here's another one."

"That's farther from where I'm digging," Lewis said. "So it's probably from one of the earlier shots, a chest shot. That would make the first one from the last shot. Sherry? Sherry?"

Sherry was sitting on the porch, elbows on her knees, crying into her hands. "I've got to go in. I'm… sorry."

"Oh, I'm so sorry, Sherry," Lewis said, helping her up onto the porch and opening the door for her. "Hey, could you get some more zip-lock bags while you're in there?" He realized immediately what he had said, as she closed the door. He heard it lock.

Lewis looked at Ted, who was shaking his head, looking down. "I can't believe you said that," Ted said.

"Me, neither. So, all in one bag, okay?"

"I don't know if makes any difference," Ted said, but let's at least get good photos that show where we found it."

"Where *you* found it," Lewis said. He took pictures and bagged the shell with the other one, just as the front door opened, and a box of zi-plocs landed on the porch. The door closed again. And locked. "She's really upset." Lewis put the second shell in a second bag, made a note on it, and laid it by the first one.

"You blame her?" Ted said, and he went back to digging along the wall, fingertips digging in the loose loam. He stopped. "Lewis, bring your phone. You're not going to like this."

Lewis stumbled around the bush, where Ted's hand was pointing to two shells. "What the hell?" was all he could say, as he tried to steady his phone to take the shot. "What the hell?"

Ted held the baggie open as Lewis loaded the shells into it. "Lewis, this isn't right. We have four shells here, and there's one in evidence."

"Yeah, and nobody heard more than four. Well, one said they heard five. Anyway, there were four shots hit Dad, and these shells are all so close together – how could he miss?"

"Did he miss? Maybe. I mean, if you're nervous. Maybe the guy didn't shoot people very often. You know, an amateur hit. That's a clue, in fact. I mean, it would probably help eliminate some suspects, like the guys from the prison. I mean, they'd know enough, if they didn't know how to do it, they'd hire somebody who did."

"Or a cop."

"You think a cop shot your dad?"

"Crossed my mind."

"Maybe somebody did some other shooting at another time."

"Yeah, from my front porch. Real likely."

"Lew, I'm just trying to make sense of this."

"I know, I know. Shit. Sorry. Now what've we got? Too much evidence. That's as bad as not enough. Maybe worse. That means…"

"Oh, crap. That means the shell they have in evidence might not be from your dad's murder."

"We better call Leonard."

"Let's keep looking for the slug. Here, use this spoon."

"Thanks… That's all the deeper you got?"

"Dude, you kept interrupting me. 'Hey, I found a shell!' 'Hey look, another shell!' Hey, go screw yourself." They both laughed, and scraped with new enthusiasm. "I'm glad you're helping here. If you'd have found one more shell…"

"Hey, here. Lewis. Something's here."

"Knock it off. It's probably a rock."

"You want to dig it out?"

"Okay. Thanks. I'm gonna use my fingers, in case it has ballistics on it."

"What?"

"In case there's those marks, get left by the barrel of the gun. It's like a fingerprint… Oh, oh shit. Oh, baby. Look, Ted."

"We'd better call Leonard. Leave it right there. Where's his card? Okay, I'll call him."

* * *

Officer Leonard arrived in twenty minutes. All three of them were sitting on the front porch, baggies in hand, and a USB stick with Lewis's cell phone shots. Lewis was thinking how small Sherry looked, sitting between them. How, as child, he had blamed her for not protecting him from his dad. But how little, how frail she must have been, even then. Leonard walked up to them, and the boys stood.

"Afternoon, Lewis, Ted, and you're, uh, Sherry? Joe Leonard. We met back when…"

"I remember you," she said. "You were thinner."

"Yeah, uh… thanks. What do you have here?"

"Well," Lewis said, "We just found a bullet here, where Sherry says my dad was lying when she found him. I think maybe it's the last shot. It was down in the dirt maybe two inches. Must've gone between the blocks. And," as he handed over the bags with the shells, "we have found four more shells, from over along the house, one in the bush there."

"Four?"

"Isn't that interesting?"

"How long have you been at this?"

Ted said, "Since we got home, straight from seeing you, so, like eight-fifteen this morning. So that's what – about four hours?"

Leonard held the bags up and looked carefully at the contents. "Well, we have to keep looking.

We have two pairs of shells here. There's two three-eighties and two nines."

"What's that mean?" Lewis was tired, frustrated

"That means we had two guns, or these shells come from two different times, maybe. It also means you're theoretically not done with looking for shells."

Lewis said, "How?"

"If it was just one incident and nobody heard more than four shots, and some heard only three, then, well, we have at best three shells that match, and you might still find the fourth."

Ted looked at Lewis, then both looked at Sherry, who shrugged.

"But," Leonard said, "you two're done for now. I'm going to call in for a team to pick up where you left off, see if there's any more shells, maybe even bullets."

He turned directly to Lewis. "And I'm going to need your cell phone."

"What? Oh, I guess I didn't tell you. That USB stick there," he said, "it has all the pictures on it."

"Thanks, but we need the originals. We'll get your phone back to you in just a few days. We won't hurt it."

"A few *days*? Look, I'm going to Mansfield on Friday morning. Can you get it back by then?

Can't you just copy it and I can pick it up, maybe like, this afternoon?"

"No can do. Friday, maybe. If not, we can mail it to you in Mansfield."

"I'll only be there for the weekend. Then I go back to school at Ohio State."

"You're a Buckeye? Great school. We can mail it to you there. But I think we can get it to you by some time on Friday." Leonard turned the phone off, then on. "What's your password?"

Lewis stumbled. "It's secret."

"Even from your roommate and your mom?"

"Sherry's not... I mean, she might as well be…"

"Your password?"

"Can I write it down for you?"

"Well, if it's that personal. Here." Leonard handed Lewis a little spiral-bound book. Lewis wrote on it, handed it back, dropped it. Sherry picked it up and handed it to the officer, barely looking at it.

"Thanks, Lewis," Leonard said. "Your password is safe with me. I'll try to get this through as fast as possible."

"It has capital and small letters and numbers, just like I wrote it. Yeah, thanks, I guess."

The police van pulled up. "Well, they're here," Leonard said. "Show us exactly where you found each thing, and then go inside. Don't come out the front door until after they're gone. We don't want anything disturbed."

"Okay," Lewis said, "but you know, it's been…"

"But this is new, even if it is a cold case and we haven't looked at anything for all this time. Now, get going, so I can get this phone back from the lab."

The trio went inside. Leonard talked with the techs for three or four minutes, then left, taking the baggies and Lewis's phone with him.

In a couple minutes, the techs rang the doorbell and talked with Lewis and Ted, saw where the shells and the bullet came from. Then they went about their business as Sherry, Ted, and Lewis watched them through the window for another forty minutes, until they left.

"What do you think?" Sherry said. "Did you see them find anything?"

"Hard to tell," Lewis answered. "It's like they don't want us to know."

Ted said, "Yeah, we did their work, now they don't want our help."

"More work for them," Lewis said. "I sure hope this helps, at least kicks them into gear to take Dad's murder seriously. How can you," he nodded at Ted, "find all that stuff in a few hours, even after years of it sitting around – and they couldn't find anything, even when it was fresh? Don't they have sniffer dogs, even? I mean, they could find fresh shell casings, right?"

Sherry looked startled. "They had a dog here. I remember."

"Must have been as stupid as that detective," Ted said.

"Makes no sense," Lewis said. "So, suppose we rich college kids take this lady out for lunch? Sky's the limit, even Denny's, if you want."

"Let's go, Mister Rockefeller," Sherry said, and she took his arm.

* * *

On the way to Mansfield on Friday, Ted first stopped at the police station. Officer Leonard met them.

"We found one more shell," Leonard said, "a nine. So that's four nines, total, including the one we found earlier."

"So, the first shell was a nine," Ted said to Lewis. Then back to Leonard, "And two three-eighties," Ted said. "What's that about?"

"We don't know if there's any connection, but we're happy to have four nines, and not likely any more of anything."

"Do the shells match the bullets?" Lewis said.

"Well, that's weird," Leonard said, scratching his head. "We can't tell if any of the shells match the bullets, but that isn't unusual. What is unusual is that five of the shells, including both three-eighties, were fired from different guns. The sixth one, we can't tell. It's too damaged."

They just stood there, looking at each other. Then Ted said, "What? Five different guns, six shots, four bullet wounds? And nobody heard more than four shots? Are you sure? I mean, what are you saying?"

"I'm saying this isn't right. I don't know what happened, but this isn't right."

"Is your lab positive? I mean, could they be making a mistake?"

Leonard said, "Ted, we didn't do a very good job on the initial investigation. I'm right with you on that, and I'm sorry. I was new, didn't think about it. But our lab – the county lab, actually, is really good. They might make *a* mistake, yes. But they wouldn't make *five* mistakes, and I don't think they're making any." He looked at Lewis, back at Ted. "This case just got a whole lot more complicated."

Lewis said, "But they can't believe there were five shooters, or six shooters – five guns – and nobody saw anything? And who brings five guys to a hit, fires one shot each? This isn't possible."

"No, it isn't," Leonard said. "The likeliest thing is that some of the shells, let's say the three-eighties, were from an earlier incident. Maybe the house's previous owner took a pot shot at a crow or something."

"Dad bought that house when my mom was pregnant with me. Those three-eighties are fifteen years older than the nines? Can they even tell?" *What's he trying to get us to swallow? Who shoots crows with a pistol?*

"They probably can tell, but I don't have that information," Leonard said. "What is really disturbing is that the shells don't look like they came from the same guns, any of them. Five guns – or three, in best-case on the nines – just don't add up."

Then he said, "Here's your phone. Thanks for the pictures. You're heading to Mansfield now?"

"Yes," Lewis said, "and thank you for letting us get involved in this, and for re-opening the case."

"It was never closed, just cold. We never give up on a murder case, not for a hundred years. Have a safe trip."

* * *

Ted had been driving in silence for an hour when he said, "What are you thinking, Lew?"

"How absolutely impossible all this is. They stop investigating almost immediately. We show up, and in half a day we found years-old evidence, right where they supposedly looked. And none of the evidence makes any sense, either."

"What do you think? Who killed your dad?"

"Well, I'd guess three different hitmen didn't. And I'd also guess that the guy who killed him didn't bring three guns. And I sure as hell don't know why they didn't find anything the first time, and why they stopped looking."

"You're still thinking a cop did it?"

"Or somebody the cops liked, like maybe one of the other prison guards. Like I said, nobody much liked my dad."

"Not a former inmate? They probably didn't like him much, either."

"Yeah, but a former inmate, the cops wouldn't give up so fast. They'd track him down. It's like a sport for them."

"Do you think the detective…?"

"I hate to think that. And he didn't retire immediately, go straight to Arizona. He hung around here, even after he retired. Didn't go to Arizona until that winter."

"Yeah, but why go in the summer?"

"Because if he killed Dad, he'd want to get out of town as fast as he could."

"Probably, yeah. It would be plenty 'hot' here. Hey, let's check when he sold his house, or at least when he put it up for sale."

"Great idea, Ted. Do you remember his name?"

"No. Can you call Leonard? I'm driving."

* * *

Back in Mansfield, Jill Hamlin was busy stripping the guest bed. No one had slept in it since Lewis left on Sunday, but she thought it would look better with fresh sheets, anyway. And it would look like she had changed it after Jack left, just in case.

In fact, Jack slept most of the days in Jill's bed, as well as the nights. "You're always asleep," Jill said.

"You wear me out all night, baby. What am I supposed to do? I want you to be happy."

"Old man, I need you conscious sometimes, too. This isn't just about the sex, you know."

"I know, baby. But if it were, it would still work for me." He laughed. She didn't.

"And for me," she said, "if it's just about the sex, once every twenty-four hours doesn't even get me started. So aren't you glad I love some other things about you, too?"

Chapter Fourteen: Dream or plan?

Jill opened the door and saw them by the porch light, coming up the sidewalk from the driveway. It was pitch dark otherwise. "I was about to call the car in stolen," she joked, as she kissed Ted and gave Lewis a hug, coming in the door. "Did you get a lot of work done for Lewis's mom?"

"Mom, Sherry's... But yes, we got a lot done. Can we eat? We'll tell you all about it."

"Right – sorry, I forget. Put your things away first. Then I'll feed you."

Lewis was back in the kitchen before Ted. "Hi, Miss Jill. I missed you. Thanks for the car, by the way."

"Missed you, too." She kissed him on the forehead. "Sit down, and you and Ted tell me what went on down in Chillicothe."

Ted walked in, grabbed a chair, sat down. Then he noticed there was nothing on the table. "Mom, what do you want me to set? Plates, all the silverware, water glasses?"

"Just sit," she said and she grabbed two diet colas from the fridge, put them on the table. "I also have some cold pizza for you. Do you want me to re-heat it?"

Ted looked at Lewis, then answered. "Cold is fine, Mom. Thanks. Sorry we're so late. I didn't know you were expecting us sooner, or any time, really."

"So here's dinner," as she put a roll of paper towels on the table and opened the pizza box, one slice missing. "I didn't wait, and I'm without a car, you know. I couldn't go shopping."

"Okay, Mom. I'm guilty. Sorry."

"I just decided to start raising you Catholic, that's all," she said, smiling. "How's the guilt trip working?"

"Perfect, Mom. I'm so guilty. I don't think I can ever make it up to you." They smiled at each other. "So why didn't you call, if you were worried?"

"Because I knew I shouldn't be worried, as long as you didn't call me," she said. "I put this all on you."

"Well, it worked." They laughed again.

"Lewis, what did you and Ted do all week?"

"We, ummm… We went to the police station, met a patrolman who worked on my dad's murder case. The detective retired, moved to Arizona…" Lewis talked for fifteen minutes straight, with only a few comments by Ted. "So we don't know if the cops were sloppy, stupid, or maybe even in on it, somehow."

"Lew thinks they know stuff they didn't tell us, stuff that isn't in the file, either. So much of this doesn't fit together. The 'dirty cop' theory might not be so crazy, but who?"

"But why would the police want to kill your father?"

"Miss Jill, nobody liked my dad. I mean, he wasn't a likeable guy. I was young – fifteen is way different from nineteen, you know -- so I don't know for sure, but they must have known what kind of husband, what kind of a father he was. I mean, he hit me a lot. He really hurt Sherry a few times. Maybe they knew what he was like. Then there were all the guys he worked with at the prison. From what I've heard, they didn't like him, either. He had several reports from where he worked in his file. They didn't show me, but they kinda told me, if you know what I mean."

"Oh, Lewis," she said.

"And there's always the chance that somebody he treated bad in prison, then got out, and he could have had a grudge. There's too many people. My dad was just a son of a bitch. Face it. He was mean." Lewis hung his head, but still reached for another slice of pizza.

"People are what they are," Jill said. "It's no reflection on you," and she put her hand gently around the back of his neck, started to give him a little massage, then stopped herself.

"Here, everybody, have another slice," she said, quickly recovered. "I'm going to make up the guest room." She left.

Ted turned to Lewis. "Don't be too hard on yourself. You couldn't stop him. You couldn't have changed him. He's just… what he was, that's all."

"Yeah, thanks. I'm going to go make up my own bed. Your mom's had a long week with that creep." Lewis walked down the hall, and Ted folded up the empty pizza box, cleaned up, and headed for his room.

As Ted was rounding the corner from the hallway into his room, his mom was coming out of Lewis's room. "Thanks for helping, Lewis," she said back over her shoulder, but Ted thought the way she said it sounded strange somehow. *And is her hair out of place, or was it like that at dinner?*

"Good night, Mom. I love you," he said, went into his room, and closed the door.

I can't stand the thought of her with that Jack, that jerk. He's such a phony. What can she see in him? Tires and brakes? She's better than that. And she doesn't know about that stunt he tried at Christmas. I hate Jack. And Ted fell asleep. He slept soundly, never hearing when she went down the hall, barefoot, in just her robe. He didn't hear her and Lewis banging the hell out of each other for the next hour, and he didn't hear her go back to her room, or hear Lewis crawl back into his own squeaky bed.

Ted woke at three-fifteen from a dream that had him sweating, his heart racing. *It's only a dream, Ted. Settle down, calm down. You didn't actually kill anybody. Jack gets to you, that's all. Tell her if you want to, but she'll think you're exaggerating, or you were misinterpreting him. You can't win this one, Ted. Leave it alone.*

He fell asleep again and slept 'til morning, but woke up groggy and irritated, as his mom and Lewis were finishing breakfast, laughing and talking.

"Hi," Ted said as he dragged himself into the kitchen. "What's so funny?"

"We were just betting on how long you'd sleep," Jill said. "You were tired last night. Then you were talking in your sleep. I tried to wake you up, but you were having none of it, so I just started breakfast alone. Then Lewis showed up."

"Coffee and bacon – two smells that I can pick up from vast distances," Ted's roommate laughed. "So I figured, why wake you up? More for me."

"Thanks, buddy," Ted said. "What did I say, in my sleep?"

"I couldn't tell," his mom said. "You were sure mad at somebody. But I couldn't make out any words." She turned to Lewis. "Does he talk in his sleep much at school?"

Ted looked at Lewis as he answered, "No, Miss Jill. I can't remember him doing that, ever." Lewis looked at Ted. "I heard you through the wall. No words. I mean, if you said anything, I couldn't make it out, but you were mad as hell at something."

"I woke you up?"

Both answered, "Yes." Then they all laughed again.

Jill asked, "Do you remember your dream?"

"Mom, I remember waking up, sweaty, mad about something, but I went back to sleep right away." *If I start saying anything, I'll spill it about Jack, and I don't want to cause trouble, and I can't cause trouble by keeping my mouth shut.* "All I remember is, I was really mad, fighting something or somebody, but I don't know what I was mad about, or who I was mad at."

"Whom."

"Whom." Thanks, Mom.

"Aren't you learning anything at college?"

"I'm learning that I didn't appreciate you enough when I was a kid."

"You mean, before September?"

"Right about then," and they laughed again.

Chapter Fifteen: Getting real

Jill drove them back to Columbus, quiet this time, thinking about how much she loved her son, how strange the relationship, *that's what it is, Jill,* with Lewis had become, how much she craved his responsive body, his good manners, his… enthusiasm. She didn't think of Jack until she had dropped the boys off and started for home.

"Lewis," Ted said as soon as they were back in their dorm room, I don't know what to do about Mom."

"What's to do about her? What she does is her business, not yours."

"She's better than that creep. He buys her a set of tires, buys me a watch, buys some groceries now and then. Then he comes to our house, brings booze…"

"You're talking about your mom, here," Lewis said.

"No, Lew. I'm talking about that asshole, that pervert. That guy, thinks he's going to be my stepdad. The hell he is. If he gets any ideas, I'll…"

"You'll what? Hire three hitmen to blow him away on your front porch? That kind of thing doesn't even happen in the movies."

"Or even in Chillicothe, I guess."

"What do you think happened to my dad?"

"You going to do any studying tonight?"

"No. Let's go to Hound Dog's, have a sandwich or something."

* * *

Over a pitcher of root beer and a fourteen-inch pizza, Lewis brought it up again. "Really, Ted. What you really think. I want to hear it. What happened to my dad?"

"Lew, I don't know. I'm going over and over this. I'm sorry. But I've got to make sense of it. The cops didn't have any clues, so they walked off. But we found all that stuff, right away. They couldn't have looked, like, for five minutes, they would have found it. Some of it, anyway."

"We don't know why it was there or when it got there, or how it got there, do we? We don't know if it was there before Dad got shot, or after. I mean, except for the bullet they found in his body, we don't know anything, really."

"What about the bullet under the paver?"

"Well, maybe. Probably. Okay, let's say that's part of it. But they can't match the bullets to any of the shells, even the shell they found right away. But let's say that shell's the real deal, too."

"Let's not, Lew. They've had it what, now, three and a half years?"

"More or less."

"Okay, in three and a half years, they haven't matched it up to that bullet, and they don't even have the gun. All they know for sure is somebody shot your dad with a nine, maybe a three-eighty.

Hit him four times – they don't know how many times he missed."

"Ted, it's worse than that. The shells didn't come from the same gun. Maybe the bullets didn't, either."

"So, where are we? Nowhere." He thought a minute. "Cop, again?"

"I didn't say that."

"This time." He poured another root beer. "Did you get the name of the detective, the one that retired?"

"Yarbrough. Clayton Yarbrough. Moved to Chandler, Arizona, summer after the murder."

"Looks like he didn't do anything on the case after maybe three weeks into it. Just packed up whatever he had, put it in that box, and went looking for his pension. Can you find him?"

Lewis said, "I already did."

"Did you talk to him?"

"Like, in a séance? He's dead. Died three weeks ago. Had a stroke two years ago, couldn't talk anyway."

"Shit." They sat there, pushing the drops of condensation down their glasses. Then Lewis started on the pitcher, only half full. He saw it as half empty tonight. He ate a gob of cheese that had fallen to the napkin in front of him. Nothing to say. "Say, Lew, can I change the subject?"

"Why not? This one's over for a while. First, I gotta hit the bathroom." He was back in two minutes. "You been in there? It's all covered with diamond plate, like they use on a school bus floor. Blue glass tile on the walls. I felt like I was peeing in a pickup truck tool box in my great-grandma's kitchen. Great atmosphere…"

"You done?"

"Yeah, sorry. What're you thinking?"

"Sherry's been, really, been your mom since you were three. She's been nice to you, right?"

"She's been great. But she's not my mom."

"But your dad, he wasn't nice to either one of you, and you still call him Dad, and, well, you don't even remember your mom, right?"

"What you saying, Ted?"

"I'm saying, Lew," and he topped up his root beer for effect, "that you have a mom who loves you that you don't call 'mom,' and a dad who…"

"A dad who didn't, right? And I still call him my dad."

"Yeah. Did you and Sherry ever talk about that? I know it's none of my business and all, but…"

"No, Ted. It's okay. I've wondered about it, myself. Dad never seemed to care, but Sherry? I mean, she never brought it up."

"Didn't you?"

"No, not really. I mean, I never saw the reason to. She called me 'Lewis,' and I called her 'Sherry.'

Never wanted to explore it that deep, I guess. You think I should call her 'Mom?'"

"I don't think you should do anything, Lew. It just seems strange to me, that's all."

"Maybe it is." Lewis got up to go, crunching the last of the ice while he was standing up. "I'm tired."

* * *

The week was rough, getting sorted out after vacation, with nothing to look forward to except finals, a month away. "It takes a week to get back on track, doesn't it, Lew?"

"At least." And Lewis was daydreaming a lot, about a girl, no, a *woman* in Mansfield. Worse, because he couldn't tell anybody, couldn't call, couldn't text. No Facebook, no nothing. Just this longing. He never thought about Nicole any more.

In Mansfield, Jill had regular weekend visits from Jack. Sometimes they would go out to dinner. But mostly he'd bring a bottle of vodka and some mix or a honey bourbon, and they'd sit on the living room couch and pretend to watch a movie, and he'd screw her once and fall asleep and snore and then go home in the morning. Late morning. And he bought her a KitchenAid mixer thing, so she could make cookies. Jack liked cookies.

* * *

"Three weeks 'til finals, Lew, and I got a text last night I'd like to talk about."

"Plenty of time for cramming later. Let me sleep. That's what Sundays are for."

Ted didn't listen. "You don't like Jack either, do you?"

"Uhhh, no."

"He hit my mom."

"WHAT?" Lewis snapped straight up in bed.

"Jack hit my mom. Last night. I got this text last night. Didn't read it until a minute ago. 'Jack hit me,' it says."

"What are you talking to *me* for? Call your mom."

Ted did. He stepped out into the hall. Nobody was up in the dorm, so nobody heard him, but Lewis saw him crying, furious, as he came back into the room five minutes later.

"Is she all right?" Lewis said, nearly shaking. "*Tell* me, dammit."

"Lew, I've gotta do something. You got any money? I mean, I don't want to eat in the cafeteria. Maybe McDonald's or something."

"Too many kids there to talk," Lewis said. "Let's walk to Tim Horton's. I'll buy."

"Okay. Get dressed. I got a lot to tell you."

* * *

Ted told Lewis how Jack had come to Mansfield, as usual. How they were watching a movie, but how Jack didn't want to talk, just booze her up and get laid, and she said she had something important to talk about, and he said they talk about the future all the time, and how that night wasn't the night to talk, and why didn't she just lie down and help him do her, and…

"She told you that?"

"I didn't want to hear it, and those weren't her exact words, but she was really wound up. He just left when I called."

"He stayed all night? She didn't throw him out?"

"He hit her. I told you. She was scared."

"Did she call the police?"

"She's calling them, as soon as she got off the phone with me. She wanted to be sure he was gone."

"Ted, this is… I don't know. This is so… Your *mom?* Oh, god."

"Lewis, I'm going to kill him."

Lewis put down his donut. "Ted? Ted! Think, man. Just take a deep breath."

Ted stood up to refill his coffee. "More?" and Lewis gave him his own empty cup. Ted put the coffees on the table and said, "Lew, I've been thinking. There has to be a way. I mean, if they can kill your dad and get away with it…"

"Ted, that's different. Cops kill people all the time, never get caught. That's 'cause they know how, they lose evidence, they ask the wrong witnesses, ask the wrong questions, stick together."

"Lew, if we stick together, we can do this, I swear. I haven't thought it all out yet, but I know there's a way. You have a gun…"

"Ted, you're talking crazy here. *I have a gun?* So we wait for him to come see your mom, pop out of the bushes, and nail him in your front yard?"

"Yeah, and we toss some shell casings around for them to find, and…"

Lewis saw Ted's face change, radically. "And what?"

"Your gun's a revolver. We don't have to toss shell casings around to confuse people. Revolvers don't throw shell casings."

"So?"

"So what if your dad was shot with a revolver, not a nine, and the killer tossed some random shell casings around, to screw with the cops?"

"Uhhh… Yeah. But – didn't Leonard say the bullets were from a nine?"

"But they're the same diameter as a thirty-eight or even a three fifty-seven, Leonard said so. Those are revolvers."

"Riiight… but the revolvers use bigger bullets. Heavier than the nine, don't they?"

Ted pulled out his phone. "Look it up. I'll do nines, you do thirty-eights. What weight was the one bullet, the 'for sure' one, the one they found…"

"In my dad? One hundred and fifteen… something. Hold on a minute. I got thirty-eights. Special, right?"

Ted mumbled, "Thirty-eight Special, yeah. Wait, I've got nines. One-fifteen or one twenty-four. What's a thirty-eight?"

"Crap. Much heavier, like one-forty-eight." Ted was still looking. "And a three-eighty's like, ninety-five. Your dad was killed by a nine."

"But you said yourself they're all the same diameter."

"They're close enough. But if it's a one-fifteen bullet, it's from a nine."

"Unless the guy makes his own ammunition. Then he loads a nine bullet into a thirty-eight. He could, couldn't he?"

"Hell, Lew, I don't know. Do I look like an ammunition specialist to you?"

"No, but I bet there's a pistol range in town somewhere here. We could go ask."

"Can we get in? Don't you have to be twenty-one?"

"Sometimes you are the dumbest guy I know. We're not going in to buy a gun. We're going in to ask a simple question."

"But what if he wants to know why we're asking?"

"School project? I don't know. What d'you want to tell him, we're investigating a possible killer-cop case?"

"Here's a place." Ted looked up from his phone. "Where is it?"

"Just south of here, couple blocks."

"Let's go," Lewis said. "I'm getting this."

"Thanks," Ted said, as he laid a five on the table for a tip.

"No tipping," Lewis said.

"Screw it, I feel like it," Ted said. "Build up some karma."

They walked south to the address… and there was nothing there. "I thought you checked," Lewis said.

"I did. Twenty-five eighty-seven. Right here."

"Yeah, Einstein, and we're looking at an alley. Great karma – you should have left a bigger tip." They laughed. "Check again. Maybe call first, they'll open just for us. Probably just don't exist on Sundays, you know, like Camelot."

"Brigadoon."

"Brigadoon, then. Who cares?" They headed back on Hudson, through the park to the river and back up to Dodridge, and then west to campus.

* * *

Still walking, and Ted pulled out his phone. "Mom? Hi… I'm with Lewis… I *am* listening. Are you okay? The cops… what? Well, sure you should… No, don't answer the phone when you know he's calling… Never, Mom. Right. Forever… I love you, too."

Lewis expected a rundown. All Ted said was, "She's getting a restraining order." And they walked back to the dorm in silence.

Chapter Sixteen: Hat trick weekend

"Jill, I've dreamed of this since I saw you walking across campus back last August, with your son. When you got into that black SUV and drove off, all I could think about was, 'Who is she?' and 'How can I see her again?' and…"

"Well, you did see me again, Charles. And now here I am, and you can see all of me you like."

He looked around the expensive hotel room, courtesy the convention where he was speaking, trying now to think of what to say next. "And you're perfect, just as I imagined. I still can't believe I ever saw you again, or especially that, here we are, making love on the top floor, almost in sight of the campus."

"Why were you downstairs?"

"Because this is where my convention is, and I'm speaking at it. The real question is why you were downstairs."

"Do you care?" she asked, and rolled over on top of him.

"Hmmm…"

"What's your name?"

Charles opened his eyes wide. "What?"

"Charles? Charlie? Chuck? And what's your last name?"

"Charles is fine. Doctor Charles Zitkowski."

"No middle name? And what kind of doctor are you?"

"Wallace. I was named after FDR's second-last vice president. Funny, if Roosevelt had died a few months earlier, Henry Wallace would have been president, instead of Harry Truman. And I'm a dermatologist.

"I'm the outgoing executive vice president of our association. Our convention starts tomorrow, and I'm kickoff speaker tonight, and I have a paper to deliver tomorrow. That's why I'm here."

Jill was holding back a smile. He caught it. "Yes, a dermatologist named Zitkowski. They called me 'Zit' before I ever got one. It's actually how I got interested in the field. And you have beautiful skin."

"Zit?" She giggled like a twelve-year-old.

"It's 'Charles,' now."

"I'm sorry, Charles. Names are funny. I don't have a middle name. Just plain old 'Jill Hamlin.'"

"Hamlin? You want to know something funny? Not 'ha-ha' funny. Ironic, funny. You know my middle name is Wallace, right?"

Jill nodded. "You just told me."

"Well, there was a guy named Hannibal Hamlin. Ever hear of him?"

"Didn't he bite some guy's face off in a movie?"

"That was Hannibal Lecter, in *Silence of the Lambs*. No, Hannibal Hamlin was Abraham Lincoln's vice president, before Andrew Johnson. He missed being president by about six weeks."

"So, we're related, like, by royalty, then?"

"Yeah, two guys nobody ever heard of today, could easily have been president, except for some close timing."

She did a little wiggle. "So let's do me again, mister vice president."

"After the kickoff, okay? There's a boring meet-and-greet buffet after. Can you stay the night tonight? Here?"

"I can come back, just go over to campus for the afternoon. When will you be back?"

"Around seven, seven-thirty. Here's the spare key. Make yourself at home. Do you want to do dinner late?"

"No, I'll go out with my son. You go give a good talk, and I'll see you tonight, Doctor… Doctor Fun."

Jill pulled on her clothes, put the bed back in order, and went down to the lobby. She called Ted from her cab. "Hi, Ted. Guess what? I'm in town. Do you have some time this afternoon to spend with your mom?"

"Hi, uh, Miss Jill. This is Lewis. Ted's at the library. Cramming for a chemistry exam. I'm just phone-sitting. Can I take a message for him?"

"Yes, tell him I called. And I'll pick you up outside Jesse Owens, by the gate, in fifteen minutes, if you're up for an interesting afternoon."

"Uhhh, Miss Jill? He's at the library. He won't make it to the stadium."

"Lewis, listen to me: tell Ted I called, that's it. Then get your own self over to the stadium gate. I'll be in a cab. Don't make me wait."

"Oh, now I get it, Miss Jill. Right away!" Then Jill called the hotel. "Yes, can you hold off doing room fourteen-eleven until five today, please? …Good. Thank you."

* * *

They went into the room. "Miss Jill, this is one fancy place. What are you doing here?"

"It's a long story, Lewis. Now, do you want to talk or what? We've got an hour."

"An hour? What if Ted calls?"

"Turn your phone off."

* * *

Half an hour later, they were headed back to campus. "Don't forget to turn your phone on, Lewis. See if Ted's been calling."

Just then, Lewis's phone rang. "Hi, Ted. Yeah, your mom called. Yeah, I picked it up. Thought it might be an emergency. Your mom's in town. Wants to know if we can meet her for dinner. She's buying. Where are you?" Lewis covered the phone and mouthed the words. "He's in the room."

Jill said, in a tiny whisper, "Tell him you'll meet him at the Union and in the meantime to call me, so I can come over in my car."

"Uhhh, right, Ted. Can you hear me okay now? Sorry. Say, now call your mom. I'm at the Union. Let me know what you decide to do."

Jill's cab dropped Lewis off near the Union. She told the driver to get her back to the hotel. Her phone rang. "Hi, Ted. Yes, I had to go through town. I was just going to leave. I'm so glad you called in time. Listen, I talked to Lewis about we're all going out for dinner if you can. Did you talk to him?"

"It's great you're here, Mom. I, Lew and I, we can be ready pretty quick. He just came in, taking a shower. I can be ready in fifteen minutes."

"Okay, you two. I'll drive by the front of your dorm in half an hour. It takes me a little while longer than you kids."

"Perfect, Mom. It'll be great to see you."

* * *

Dinner didn't take long. No crowds on Sunday night. She was back at the hotel by six-fifteen. The room was all made up. Jill took a shower, laid out her clothes for morning, and put on a diaphanous black-lace nightgown.

She pushed back the full-length curtain and opened the glass door to the balcony overlooking the atrium, from where she could see people, some in suits, some in polo shirts and shorts, milling about, circling stainless-steel steam trays full of rubber chicken and other convention favorites. She wished she could go down there and take a glass of champagne from one of the silver trays everybody seemed to be offering.

She walked over to the bed and sat down. Then she stretched out on top of it and fell asleep for half an hour.

* * *

"Doctor Fun, at your service." He was back, he was buzzed, and she was awake. He took off his jacket and laid it over the chair's back, kicked off his shoes, pulled off his necktie and dropped it on the floor.

Jill walked over to him and unbuttoned his shirt, pulled it back behind him, cufflinks not letting his hands go free. She yanked at his belt and pulled his trousers to the floor. He stepped out of them. She pulled his shorts down, too. All he had on was his shirt, holding his hands behind his back. He was play-struggling to get the cufflinks out. He freed one hand, she pushed him down on the bed, and he threw his shirt, still covering one arm, over her head, as his other hand went down and pulled her nightgown up.

They were both naked, except his arm was still in the shirt and Jill had his shirt and her nightgown wrapped around her head.

And they had sex, just that way, and then lay there on their backs, laughing and exhausted, pulling off the wadded clothing and tossing it… somewhere, then pulling the bedspread over themselves and rolling themselves up tight in it, off the bed and onto the floor, Charles on the bottom, still laughing.

"So, it was a good keynote?" Jill said.

"And you had a good dinner with your son?"

Charles didn't snore. When the wake-up call came, they were still on the floor, still wrapped in the bedspread.

Jill opened her eyes. "Once more?"

Charles stood up. He extended his hand down to her, and with a powerful but gentle gesture, he helped her to her feet. And he immediately pushed her down onto the bed. "It's a shame to not give housekeeping something to do," he said, as they played one more round before he went to the shower.

When he returned, wearing a hotel towel, Jill was on the way back to Mansfield.

Charles turned his phone back on and dialed. "Jessica? Hi, baby doll. Yes, daddy's boring convention is over. Does my little girl have time to see her daddy for lunch, or maybe the whole afternoon?... Yes, I know you're a sophomore now… Great. I'll be there in half an hour."

* * *

She was annoyed as she fished in her purse for her cell phone and answered Jack's call. "What?"

"Listen, baby. Jill, I can't tell you how sorry I am. I wasn't myself, and I'll never do anything like that again. I would rather die than hurt you."

"Well, you did. And if you'd rather die, then please do." And she hung up. She didn't answer when it rang immediately after, either. *Left a damn message. Crap! Now he's texting. Son of a bitch.* She turned her phone off, turned on the oldies station, loud, and kept driving.

Jill was exhausted when she pulled into her driveway. Her first solo weekend out had been a success, meeting Charles. *He certainly seemed interested. Think I'll find out a little more… And that Lewis – what will I do with that boy?* She chuckled, but she was embarrassed to answer herself.

Anything I want. Is that selfish? I mean, he's getting what he wants, too. What else does a boy that age want? And I know I'm not bragging when I say he's getting better than he'd ever find on campus, with those girls…

Jill felt better, maybe even a little smug, as she opened the door and dropped her overnight bag on the floor.

She walked into the kitchen and fired up the television on the counter, opened the fridge and heated some leftovers, picked at them a little. *Doctor Charles Zitkowski. Wonder who he is, really, besides my age, good-looking, famous…*

She turned on her phone and Jack's message was there: *So sorry. Never have another drink in my life. Promise. I love you.*

She googled Dr. Charles Zitkowski, M.D. *Hmmm… Age, forty. Former Executive Vice…*

Schooled University of Rochester... Lives in Chicago, plastic surgery practice,... wife and three children...

She started in on herself. *Nice one, Jill. You sure can pick 'em.*

And she poured half a glass of Jim Beam over a couple ice cubes, then started unpacking.

Half the drink gone, and her phone rang. "What?"

"Baby, it's me. Did you get my text? My message? I'm through. I mean it. No more drinking, never again."

"Shut up, Jack. Just come here and hold me."

He stumbled, confused. Swallowed. Then he said, "What's wrong?"

"I don't want to talk about it. Can you come over, spend the night with a sad little woman who's feeling sorry for herself?"

"Jill, are you okay? Is Ted…?"

"We're all fine." She regrouped. "So, are you coming over or not?"

"I'll be there before dark. Jill, baby?"

"What?"

"I love you."

"Just get here."

* * *

Lewis was running things over in his mind. He turned to Ted. "Did your mom come down here just to see you?"

"I doubt it. She would have called to check would I be here or was I having a test. Funny, though. She didn't say, and I didn't ask her."

"She never did that last year."

"Yeah, I know. I was here, remember? So, Lew, speaking of mysteries, what do you think happened to your dad? Do you think somebody loaded up special ammo, just to throw off the police? I mean if he did, why would the shells be so random?"

"Yeah, the perfect crime, and then he blows it with the shells. Or…"

"You're still thinking a cop did it."

"Some kind of pro. I mean, would a regular guy off the street who decides to shoot somebody go to all the trouble of making special ammunition? No. He'd just buy a box of something at Walmart, or have a friend buy it for him."

"But somebody who knew what he was doing would know about the shell casings. I mean, why would he throw two sizes of shells? And the wrong number, too?"

"Or he's a pro who wants to make it look like an amateur did it. No, he'd still use the right shells. Damn it, Ted, it doesn't make sense. Do you suppose it doesn't make sense on purpose?"

"Lewis, there's another possibility. Maybe somebody who knew very little was using the pro's special ammo."

"Ted, wait. You mean reloader-man who makes thirty-eight Special ammo using nine-millimeter bullets gives his special setup to the killer and says, 'don't forget to scatter some shells around when you off the guy.'"

"So now you've got two people wanting to kill your dad, a pro and an apprentice or something."

"Yeah, like the Beltway Sniper, John Muhammad. Remember, he had that kid do the actual shooting. He was training the kid, but the kid probably didn't load the ammunition, measure the distances, all that. The pro says, 'Here, use this gun and remember to toss some brass,' just to throw everybody off?"

"So where does the apprentice get the shells? At the range. Just picks 'em up off the floor. But he doesn't put 'em in the recycling pail. He puts 'em in his pocket, takes 'em home."

"But that doesn't work."

"What's wrong with that, Lew?"

"Because the pro, he's going to want to see the shells, make sure everything's just right. The shooter won't see the difference between nines and three-eighties, but the pro will."

"Lew, you're right. So why?…"

"Maybe they were out of time. My dad's changing shifts, or the killers are splitting up, heading out of town…"

"Like to Arizona? That what you're thinking?"

"It always comes back to a dirty cop, no matter how many times I go over it in my head. Maybe I'm just missing something, but what?"

"Let's ask Leonard if that detective, what's his name…"

"Yarbrough. Clayton Yarbrough. I'm never going to forget that name. I should hate him. He killed my dad, but still, he actually helped me and Sherry, really a lot. Face it, I wouldn't be here without the life insurance."

"Geez, Lewis. That's cold. Anyway, let's find out if anybody knows if Detective Yarbrough loaded his own ammunition."

* * *

"Yes, tell him it's Lewis Foreman, please… Hello, Officer Leonard? Hi. It's Lewis Foreman… Had a great weekend. You? Great. Hey, do you know, or does somebody know if Detective Yarbrough might have been a gun nut, maybe loaded his own ammo?... Yes, thanks, Officer. Just a hunch. Thanks."

Lewis turned to Ted. "Well…"

"Well, what?"

"Leonard didn't know him that well, but he asked an old timer, right there. Said Yarbrough was a straight-arrow, didn't like guns. The only thing he would have used was his issued duty weapon."

"Even if he's killing somebody?"

"Ted, I didn't ask him that. But from the sound of that guy – I heard him in the background – Yarbrough never broke a reg in his life. I'm thinking we're wrong. He's not the killer."

"You don't think Leonard?…"

"Oh, god, no. But it's somebody the cops like, at least. Not Yarbrough. The whole case is just too full of bad work. I mean, hell, even us – a couple of underclassmen – even we can see there's a bad job on this."

"Lew, maybe they were just busy. They have other cases, you know. And if, well, if nobody's pushing them on this one, they get another one, then another. Then it's an old case, nobody remembers anything, they don't know anything, and it just goes to the bottom of the pile."

"But he was my dad…"

"But who really missed him? …Oh, Lew, sorry. That was over the top. Sorry, man. Really."

"Oh, stuff it, Ted. I'm just curious, and if I have any regrets, it's that I don't know whose hand to shake."

"Sherry? How does she feel?"

"She should have divorced him. He was awful to her."

"Doesn't she miss him?"

"We don't talk about Dad."

* * *

"Where are you, Jack?"

"I'm at the end of your street."

"Why aren't you here?"

"Because, dear Jill, I have a restraining order against me. I can't come within a thousand feet of you. I'm probably in violation right where I am, in the car."

"Oh, for god's sake, Jack. I was mad. I tore it up as soon as I got it. I just wanted you to know I won't take any more crap from you."

"So I can come up the driveway? There's no S.W.A.T. team in your back yard?"

"Jack, get your ass over here, now."

* * *

Jack, true to his word, didn't drink. But Jill did; Jack poured.

Jill was exhausted, tired, depressed. *Why do I even want sex when I feel like this?* She had no ready answer, so she asked it out loud. "Why do I even want sex when I feel like this?" Jack looked at her, waiting. She had more questions, maybe even an answer. "Do you think I'm too much about sex?"

"If you are, well," he smiled at himself, then realized he was about to dig a hole. "If you are, baby, there has to be a good reason for it. What do you think it is – I mean, if you think you're too much about sex?"

"My whole life." She took another sip, draining the glass. She handed it back to Jack, who refilled it. "My whole life has been sex, sex, sex."

"Why?" the clumsy man said, mostly just wanting to get to it rather than listen about it.

"I, …I guess it's about being accepted. I wasn't 'pretty' in high school. Skinny, shy. Nobody asked me out. I stayed away from boys."

Jack moved closer on the sofa. Jill burst into tears, held out her glass. Jack put the glass on the table, leaned in, held her. "Now, baby, it's all right. Lots of girls are shy when they're kids."

"No, you dope. I hated boys, men, especially. I lost my virginity when I was twelve, and it sure as hell wasn't my idea." She pushed him away, reached over, picked up her drink. "My father's friend down the street, he had a son, high school, a junior."

"So, what…"

"Shut up and listen," she said, "and fill this." He obeyed, leaned back.

"My dad's friend and his slack-jaw son came over one Saturday afternoon to see if they could borrow some tool or something from my dad, but I told them he wasn't home. Just me, and I was doing my homework. The guy said 'Brett here, he's real smart. He'll help you with your homework,' then to the son, 'Won't you, Brett?' And the dad pushed me down the hall, with his son following, saying, 'Yeah, I know all the stuff you're learning. I already learnt it.' And I ran away into my room and locked the door.

"But they didn't go away. Brett just said, 'Let me help you,' and his dad said, 'You can learn a lot from the two of us,' and they wouldn't go away. And the dad, he just pushed on my door – those doors were real cheap and flimsy – and it popped open, and they pushed me onto the bed. The old man, sweaty, hairy, bad breath – I remember that awful breath – he held me down while Brett pulled his pants off, kicked off his shoes.

"Then, this was weird. Then, Brett sat on me as his dad took off his clothes. 'Age before,' he started to say, then, 'oh, fuck it. Brett, you just watch this, and you do it like I show you.' And Brett held my hands up over my head as his disgusting father raped me. And then Brett raped me, too."

Jack's expression was frozen. Jill took another sip, kept going. "So, I hated men. For years. Then I decided I wanted to get even, make men fall in love with me, then kick them out the door, break their hearts. It was easy. I really did break a lot of hearts. And I started liking sex, when I was in charge. And I was *always* in charge. I liked the sex, a lot. But I *loved* the power it gave me."

"Then, when you met Ted's father?" Jack asked.

"When I met the man I married, Ted's father…"

"He have a name?"

"Not tonight, not for the part of the story I'm telling you," she said. "When I met Ted's father, he wasn't all that interested. I don't know if he knew my reputation and like it, or if he was afraid of me. But he was nice. He was kind. He didn't try to jump me, and for some reason, I didn't want to just fuck him and get rid of him. Actually, it took me a long time to get him to like me, to trust me…

More." She held out the glass, tipping it back and forth.

"But after two years – remember, I was still *really* young – after two years, I got him to propose. And that was the only relationship I ever had, that was based on love."

"The only one?"

"Pretty much, yes." She took anoither sip. "Oh, Jack, I like you. You're a nice man. But I'm still… I'm still me, I guess. I don't want to hurt you, but I don't want to, you know… I hope that's okay with you."

And he snored all night, after they had sex. They didn't say six more words to each other. Just did it and fell asleep. In the morning, Jill made coffee and toast.

Jack was halfway home when he called her. "Baby, thanks for taking me back."

"You're not *back*, Jack. I just needed you last night."

"Want to talk about it?"

"No. Maybe in fifty years. Remind me. Drive safe."

"Baby? One more thing. You know, once you invite me over, that restraining order is cancelled."

"If I ever need another one, I'll cancel you myself. Now put down the phone and drive."

"'Bye, baby. I love you."

"'Bye."

Chapter Seventeen:
Little question, big answer

Ted's phone beeped. The call was over. "Lew," he said, "she's let him back in the house."

Lewis was studying, not listening to Ted's conversation. "Who let who back in whose house?"

"Mom let *whom* back into our house, you mean." He laughed, trying to slow down Lewis's adrenaline. It didn't work.

"You're shitting me. Jack's back?"

Ted nodded. "She's been seeing him for a few weeks. 'Didn't want to upset me while I'm studying,' she says. Well, I'm upset now. That bastard."

"Is he being good to her?"

"Hell, I don't know. He'd better be. At least Mom says he's stopped drinking."

"That's good, at least."

"No. She says she has to drink more, thinking he's not really changed."

"So he's getting her drunk whenever he sees her? Nice guy."

"That's my mom, and I thought that guy was gone. I hated him enough before. Now I think I hate him even more. I mean, if mom's drinking, that means…"

"That means he's… that just means I hate him, too. Ted, remember when we talked about… Were you serious? I mean, literally serious?"

"I don't know, Lew. I mean, that's… that's about as much 'crime' as you can commit. Get caught, and your life is over, too."

"Well, you answered my question, anyhow."

"What do you mean?"

"You're already into it. All you're worried about is getting caught. You just said so."

"Cripes, Lew. You're right."

"So let's us not get caught. I'm in. Now, we gotta think."

"You mean, get Jack away from my mom?"

"Permanently. Whatever it takes. And your mom can't know, because she's acting confused, might change her mind. I mean, she's seeing him again, right? That's nuts."

"Lew, you still have that gun?"

"The one you told me to leave at Sherry's?" He looked guilty.

"Great. Don't tell me where it is. But maybe we can use it."

"Ted, what gun?"

"Right. The one I never saw and don't know anything about."

"Don't know what you're talking about."

They were getting into the game, the game that wasn't a game.

* * *

Ted put his phone on speaker, which jerked Lewis away from his biology book. "So, Ted," it was Jill's voice and Lewis was listening, "we're going to spend Halloween weekend in Columbus."

"That's great, Mom. So, Friday night and Saturday night?"

"Yes. I can come in on Friday afternoon, if you would like to see me, maybe have time to take me downtown. I'll buy dinner. Lewis, too, of course, if he can make it."

Ted raised his eyebrows, and Lewis said, "I'm open on Friday, Miss Jill. All day. And I'd love to come with you. And Ted, of course." He laughed. So did Ted.

Ted took the conversation back. "So, Jack gets in Saturday?"

"Afternoon, so if you want to have an uptown breakfast, we can get together for that, too."

"And Saturday night?" Ted wanted to know if he was part of the plan.

"Oh, I'm sure you and Lewis will be partying on Saturday night. I won't bother you. But if you'd like to see Jack on Saturday afternoon…"

"No, thanks, Mom. That's okay. I'll probably be seeing him at Thanksgiving again. Or Christmas. You have a good time."

"Okay, Ted. So I'll call you when I know where and when, exactly. Love you!"

"I love you, too, Mom." Everybody hung up. Ted looked at Lewis. "You think?"

"Lewis said, "Let's do it. Halloween, night of the dead. Perfect."

* * *

"Ted, something strange happened this afternoon. Sherry called, said she was feeling lonesome, kinda for no reason."

"That is strange. Does she want you to visit?"

"Didn't say. Just sounded really down. Maybe I should get a bus home, spend a weekend. Weird – she never was lonesome last year. I mean, I was, homesick and all. Never been away. But this year is different. I'm in a groove, and I would've thought she'd be, too."

"Lew?"

"What?"

"I've got an idea. Halloween's two weekends away. Do you think she could hold out 'til then? We could have a real party, with Sherry and my mom both here…and Jack, but she wouldn't meet Jack. He doesn't get in until Saturday. It'd be fun."

"Ted, Sherry doesn't have any money. Hotels…"

"Lewis, how much can they be? I mean, sure, the ritzy place – but Jack's paying for that, I'll bet anything. I mean, why can't we – I'll pay half – we'll pay for Sherry's. Just ask her, please?"

* * *

Sometime in the middle of the night. "Hey, Ted?"

"Trying to sleep. What?"

"Why don't you tell your mom about Jessica?"

"Why don't you leave all that alone? You know, you've been weird ever since Nicole didn't come back."

"Wrong, bro. I was weird way before that."

"Get another girlfriend. Or something. Just let me sleep."

"Okay. Sorry. G'night."

"Just shut up, you horny bastard."

Chapter Eighteen: Halloween, part I

"This is great, gentlemen," Sherry said, "and it's so wonderful finally to meet you, Jill. The boys talk about you a lot."

"Likewise, Sherry. I don't know why we haven't gotten together before."

"Well, Mom, it's like, either we have a family holiday, or there's exams, or everybody's busy with some project or something, or…"

"Oh, stop it, Ted. We're all here now, having dinner in the noisiest restaurant in Ohio, and it's great. All four of us, like an extended family."

Lewis said, "Sherry, haven't I told you a lot about Ted's mom? She's really nice, isn't she?"

Sherry laughed. "Yes, and she's very pretty, too. For a mom."

As Jill pretended to blush, Lewis and Ted said in unison, "For a mom." They all laughed again.

"You obviously spend a lot of time together, don't you?" Sherry said. "Do you always plan everything together?"

Lewis said, "I don't know if the word is 'plan,' exactly. We just sort of know each other's schedule, and we like doing the same things, mostly, so it just works out."

Jill said, "Do you boys have any plans for, after graduation? What you want to do? Have you picked out some companies, maybe where you'll be interns next summer?"

Ted and Lew looked at each other, and Ted said, "No."

Lewis quickly said, "But we should, for sure. It just seems like, you know, college is forever. But you're right – in a couple years, we'll be out of here. I mean, two years ago, that was junior year. That seems like a different world. But it was just two years ago."

"And two years from now," Ted said, "is going to come up pretty quickly. I mean, I feel like I just started college, and here I am, middle of sophomore year." He looked straight at his mom. "And there is a lot to plan, short term and long term. It's all up to me now." He looked to Lewis.

"You're spoiling the mood here, Ted. It's Halloween. We don't have anything to plan except this weekend. Then back to the real world, okay?"

Jill looked at Sherry. "Hey, would you like to come back to my hotel? It's got unlimited cable. It's also a lot quieter than this place, and private. I'm sure there's plenty we can talk about if we can hear each other."

"Great idea, Jill. I'm parked just around the corner. Lewis and I can follow you and Ted." She looked at Lewis. "And if we get lost, I'm sure you know Ted's number."

Jill's Taurus led the way to the Castella Diamonte, a swanky new building with an art deco look that seemed out of place. The valet took her car, and Jill got out and motioned Sherry to pull up. "These are my guests," she told the valet. "Not staying the night, so park it so they can get it out." He nodded at the twenty dollar bill she gave him and returned a big smile.

"I didn't know this was here," Sherry said, as they entered room nine-oh-six and admired the view. "And so close to campus. What is it, two miles?"

Lewis looked out the window, counting streets as he looked northwest. "Two miles is just about exact, to our dorm," he said. Are your initials really GPS?"

Jill said to Sherry, "How about a bottle of champagne to celebrate this little get-together?"

"I'd go for it," she said, "but Ted and Lewis…"

"We don't need any," Ted said, as Lewis playfully kicked him, obviously having fun. "We don't want you ladies contributing to our delinquency."

They laughed, but Jill and Lewis seemed to look at each other's smiles just a little longer. Sherry noticed but pretended not to.

Lewis said, "I'll run down to the machines and get us some Mountain Dew." He looked at Jill. "Do they have machines here?"

Jill looked in the *Things We Do For You* menu on the television table. Back page. "There's a set of machines in the lobby," she said, "and here – another set on the fifth floor."

"I'll be back in a flash," Lewis said.

Ted said, "I'll go with you," and they left Sherry and Jill to talk about them.

In the hall. "Lewis, look for cameras, but don't be obvious. You take the elevator. I'll take the stairs, meet you at the vending machines."

At the machines, Ted said, "There's cameras in each turnaround, you know, between floors, but if you look down, they can't see your face. But they would if you were coming up, looking up."

"No camera in the elevator, not that I could see," Lewis said, "but there's one directly across from the elevator door. Sees your back when you get on, but it's looking straight at you when you get off. It's there at the sign that says 'this way to room so-and-so,' so you look right at it."

"Gotta remember not to come straight out, keep from looking across the hall when you go in," Ted said.

"So they saw us plenty tonight."

"So, Lew? Today, we're getting Mountain Dew, dressed for our moms, er, our…"

"Skip it. I get it. Tomorrow we look like college kids."

"Sunday."

"Sunday. See, they have a big buffet on Sundays. I saw the sign. I know Mom will do her routine – get a shower, go down and heap up a plate for him, get something for herself, and bring it back to the room. They'll munch on it 'til noon."

"Noon?"

"Checkout time. So, we go in to talk to Jack while she's getting the food. We'll have a minute or two, maybe five – depends when we see her go down for the food. But we'll count on two minutes, to talk some sense into that jerk."

"You only want to talk to him? What do I need to bring Dad's gun for?"

"So he'll listen and take us seriously. Besides, you won't be holding it. This is personal, him and me. Keeps you out of it."

Back at the room with a couple cans of Mountain Dew. One knock, Jill said, "Door's open," and they spent a lovely time, the four of them. Sherry volunteered to drive back to campus.

"But first," Lewis said, "Let's make sure you know how to get around, to your hotel. We'll go there first, together, make sure you're all checked in and set."

"Oh, Lewis, you're treating me like a celebrity."

Ted said, "We wanted you to be able to stay over, not drive back to Chillicothe after such a wild party."

"Well, I thank the both of you," she said. Then, "Is this it? Is it made up for Halloween?"

"Uhhh… This might be it. GPS says so." The place was dreadful. "Ted, see if this is the right place. Ask Siri or Google or somebody."

"What's the address? Dude, we're on South High Street. The hotel's on North."

Sherry tried to be nice, but she was clearly relieved. "Well, that gives us another chance. Let's see what the real place is like."

It wasn't bad. Not scary. Clean. Basic. Free parking, too. "Thank you, gentlemen," Sherry said, as she dropped them off at the dorm ten minutes later. "I had a great time with you, and your mom's so nice, Ted. No wonder Lewis is always talking about her."

"Good night, Missus Hobart," Ted said. "Thanks for the ride." Then as she drove off, he turned to Lewis. "*Always talking about her?* Man, give it up, or I'm keeping your gun after this weekend."

Lewis laughed. But he was nervous, a little.

Chapter Nineteen: Intermission

Saturday morning nine-thirty, and Ted's phone rang. "Can I pick you boys up for breakfast?"

"Hey, Lewis. Want to go to breakfast with me and my mom?... Half an hour? Great." He turned to Lewis, who was lying on his bed, groggy, holding a pillow over his head. "The only reason in the world I would put a wolverine in your pillowcase is coming to take us to breakfast in half an hour. Get yourself up."

As they got ready, Lewis said, "So, how are we going to do this? Have you been thinking? Did you see the cameras in the lobby?"

"Yeah, there's a lot of 'em at the entrance and by the desk, another one like the other ones, across from each elevator. The parking lot entrance has one, too, halfway down the hall. Gotta keep our heads down."

"What about in the parking lot?"

"Crap. I didn't see out there. We're going to have to get a better look from a distance."

Lewis said, "Maybe your mom would like to see some of the pictures we've been taking around here. You know, like on a slide show. You can show her them on your computer while I scout around."

"You mean, like, we go back to her hotel after breakfast?"

"Yeah. You keep her busy for half an hour. I find out everything."

"That'd work. Just don't be obvious about what you're looking at, and don't be shy about being seen by the cameras. Just be natural."

"Yes, Ted. And I won't jack off in public, either. Got any more advice?"

"No, that about covers it. You got any pictures organized anywhere?"

"I'll get 'em together. You just get your shower. You've got five minutes. Then me. Then we'll stall her if we need to."

"How about I call her and get another fifteen minutes?"

"Yeah, do it. I know I can get it done in that much time."

* * *

"Hi, Mom. Lew and I will be right down." He hung up and turned to his roommate. "Got a nice long slide show?"

"As long as you can keep talking, bro. Let's go. I'm all charged up." He patted his computer. "Anything up to three, four hours."

Jill reached across the front seat and opened the door as Ted got in. "I always thought it was us girls, taking the extra time to get ready," she said.

"We have a surprise for you, Miss Jill," Lewis said, "If you have time after breakfast."

"What's the surprise?"

Ted rolled his eyes. "Mom, it's not a surprise if we tell you. Can we go back to the hotel after breakfast, maybe half an hour is all it will take. Are you busy after breakfast?"

"Well, it must be good. Sure. I mean, what else would I be doing? Sitting watching cable, lying around. I'd love some company after breakfast. What have you and Lewis cooked up?"

"You'll see," said Ted.

* * *

Back at the hotel, eleven in the morning. Housekeeping had freshened everything up. The lady was leaving just as they went in the ninth-floor room.

"Okay, Mom. Lewis actually did these shots, so we're going to explore this together." Ted opened the computer and stuck Lewis's flash drive in. The show was starting.

"These aren't in any particular order, Miss Jill. They're just some of my better shots. Mostly campus, some of the park, some of downtown, and a couple of my house and your house, too."

They looked at a dozen shots, all mixed up, a real hodgepodge of architecture, blurry photos of dorm life, pictures of rainstorms shot through the windows of various buildings, somebody they couldn't identify at a restaurant. "I don't know who that is," Lewis said, "but she was framed so well – you see that wooden arch? – I just had to take the picture."

"You're a good photographer, Lewis," Jill said, lying. She was going to say, "You certainly take a lot of artsy pictures," but she thought he might take that the wrong way, the way she actually meant it.

Lewis stood up. "Ted, can you keep the show going? I'm going to go get some Mountain Dew. You want one? You, Miss Jill?"

Ted said "Thanks."

His mom said, "No thanks. Diet something? With caffeine?"

"I'll see what I can do." Lewis was gone. Ted carried on, narrating or making up stories for each of the pictures, dragging the show on for as long as his mom could take it. Finally, after about ten minutes, she said, "Where is your roommate? Did he get lost or something?"

Ted stood up, looked out the window, and saw Lewis in the parking lot. "I can't figure what happened," he said. "Maybe he had to go get change or something, or maybe the machine was out of diet or Mountain Dew."

"How hard is it to get change?" she said. "I mean, is he walking back to your dorm room?" They laughed. Ted moved away from the window, sat down next to his mom.

"Can you stand another couple pictures?"

"Did he take any good ones?"

"Let's find out... Sorry, Mom, I didn't ever see most of these. Yeah, he's not Ansel Adams, that's for sure. But at least you're getting a pretty good idea of everyday life on campus."

Two more pictures. Then out of nowhere, "Mom, why are you still seeing Jack?"

She hesitated, then said, "Ted, it's complicated. You know about that, that time. The restraining order. He was drinking. He was sorry, really sorry. Crying, sorry."

"Mom, you drink too, and you don't go around hitting people. 'Sorry?' Of course he's sorry. He's lucky you didn't press charges."

"First of all, Theodore." She never called him Theodore unless something big was about to happen, "How much I drink isn't your business or anybody's business. I handle it. I never drink and drive. I never black out. I haven't even had a hangover in ten years. It's not your business, son of mine.

"Secondly, I can read men. Jack's a good man, deep down. Nobody's perfect, but he thinks of me."

"Mom, a set of tires is pretty basic. It's not romantic like, uhhh, like..."

"Like a thousand-dollar wristwatch?"

"I didn't want to say that, but, well, yes. He's weird, Mom. I don't like him. But worse, he hit you. I can't trust him, and especially with you. Mom, you're all I've got in this world. I'm worried."

Ted closed his eyes, forcing a tear, and Jill drew close to him, stroking the hair on the back of his head, holding his hand. And Lewis knocked on the door.

"Here's the drinks," he said. Then he looked at Ted. "What's up, man? Were the pictures that bad?"

Jill said, "They'll be better when we're all dead, I'm sure, Lewis. You know, collectible. But they were interesting. Very, you know, unpretentious. Very lifelike. Earthy. Maybe you'll get famous, like Picasso, cut off your ear…"

Ted tried to hold back, but Lewis made a face at him, and he burst into laughter. Jill looked at him. "What?"

"Mom, that was Van Gogh, not Picasso." He was in tears. "Lew, give me that Dew."

Jill looked at Lewis. "It wasn't that funny," she said.

Ted made a face at Lewis, and the roommate blurshed out some Mountain Dew through his nose, took off for the bathroom, holding the can and trying to catch the drops in his other hand.

Ted was under control, but gasping for breath. "Mom, that was great. We had that Van Gogh thing in class, just this week. Perfect timing."

Lewis, face looking flushed, came back into the room. "Sorry, Miss Jill. Really, we learned about Van Gogh and his ear this week. We were supposed to guess why he did it. One of the guys said, 'So he could get famous?' That was perfect. Sorry again, really."

"Well, unless you're going to cut your ear off, you can stay, and I'll look at the rest of the pictures."

"No, Mom, I think we're just as well off, leaving," Ted said. "I'm sorry, too, but hey, it was funny!" He looked at Lewis and they started laughing again. This time, Jill joined them.

"Okay, boys, let's go. Down to the car."

* * *

Back in the room, Lewis said, "Didn't see a single camera anywhere covering the parking lot itself. Cameras under the portico, by the valet thing, and a camera coming in both entrances, but not anywhere else. Next door, there's a camera on a light post that might get a view of the front door. It looks like the only cameras we have to plan for are the ones we spotted yesterday."

"Okay, let's get our clothes ready. What did you wear yesterday?"

"Hell, Ted, I don't know. Why does it matter?"

"Uhhh, because you were on camera yesterday?"

"Yeah, I get it. None of yesterday's clothes or today's."

"Did you wear the same shoes yesterday?"

"Yeah, I think so," Lewis said.

"Then let's think this through. Nothing that's been on camera. You still have that hoodie?"

Lewis nodded. "Wear that. And your beat-up Nikes, jeans. Nothing that draws attention. Jeans without holes or stains, no patterns."

"Okay, I'll get that stuff ready. What are you wearing?"

Ted said, "I wore this exact outfit yesterday." Lazy. And it was still clean. "I'll wear that Ohio State sweatshirt and that baseball hat. Sunglasses, if it's sunny. You got sunglasses?... Wear 'em. No, bring them, put them on when we get close to their cameras."

"Anything else?" Lewis said. He was setting out tomorrow's clothes.

"Yeah, something else to wear, 'til we're off campus. Rain pants and jacket – something that will cover, and you can roll it up and put it in your pocket, or just leave it with the bikes. We're only going to be there a few minutes, but we don't want somebody on campus seeing us in the videos and recognizing us by the clothes."

"How about this?" Lewis held up a faded Ohio State hoodie.

"Perfect," Ted said. "Yeah, that one. And one other thing. Bring your dad's gun."

"You crazy?"

"Just give it to me," Ted said. I'll just use it to keep him at a distance, paying attention."

"Ted, you're not going to shoot him. Are you?"

"I have no such plan. Only to make him remember what I'm going to tell him."

"Which is?"

"Which is, 'Stay away from my mom, and stay away from me,' and I want it to sink in real good."

"Ted, promise me you won't shoot him."

"Okay, I promise. I mean, unless he makes me somehow."

"Promise."

"Okay, Lewis, I promise I won't shoot him."

"Or anything else, like some stupid warning shot over his head."

"Or anything else. Promise." Lewis looked relieved. Ted said, "So remember your dad's gun in the morning. I'll carry it. And you know how to get into the parking lot and where to put the bikes? No cameras all the way, right?"

"Invisible. But you're not going to shoot him, remember. You promised."

"I promise, Lew. Now let's go over this again..."

* * *

"So, Sherry, don't worry. I'll take care of it." Jill was watching the parking lot as Jack's Buick pulled in. "Listen, I've got to go. But I'll meet you for breakfast. I really have to talk with you." Jill stashed her phone in her purse, checked her lipstick, walked across the suite."Jack," she said as she opened the door. "I..."

"Jill, my beautiful Jill," he said, as he swept into the room, a dozen roses in one hand and a magnum of champagne in the other.

"Jill, baby, how I've missed you."

"Jack, it's only been three weeks," she said. "And what's this for? You said you stopped drinking. But the roses," and she took them out of the box and looked for something to put them in, didn't find anything, and put them on the window sill, "these are gorgeous!" And she threw her arms around him, big kiss, dragged him to the couch and pulled him down on her.

"I'll call down for an ice bucket, Goldilocks. Are there some of those elegant wrapped-up plastic cups in the bathroom?"

"Jack, you said you stopped drinking. Now you're asking for champagne glasses."

"Champagne's not 'drinking,' baby. It's 'celebrating.' Just this one night. It's special for us, you know. A milestone." And he glanced over at the roses, one of them now on the floor below the window. Made his puppy-eyes at her.

"Oh, get the damned ice," she said. "I'll get changed." And she went into the bedroom.

"Don't change too much," Jack called out. "I like you the way you are."

Oh, god. And he's not even drinking. I need him gone, but well, I agreed, and he's like a little kid, all enthusiastic, goofy. Maybe let's see how it goes.

"Ice is on the way, baby."

I'm so damned sick of hearing, 'baby.' She said, "I'll be out in a minute."

Chapter Twenty: Halloween, part II

"Okay, Lewis, you ready?"

"Ready as I'm ever going to be," he said. "Here's the gun. Remember, you promised."

They took separate paths to their bikes, and different routes to the hotel. Lewis arrived first and peeled off his outer layer of clothes, stashing them in a plastic garbage bag under a rock at the edge of the parking lot, out of sight of the cameras. He chained up his bike, leaving the combination with just one number yet to be dialed in, for a quick escape. He turned around and saw Ted circling in from another direction. "Ready?"

Ted said, "Let's do this." They walked to the rear entrance, Ted entering first and heading to the stairwell, cap on, head down. Lewis pulled up his hood and kept his face down, too, and they regrouped at the first landing, directly under and out of range of the camera. Two thumbs up, and keeping their heads low, they climbed to the ninth floor.

Ted cracked the door and waited. Fifteen long minutes went by. *One health nut decides to walk down the stairs. That's all it would take, and we're screwed.* "Lewis, this could take a while," he whispered. Let's get comfortable." They both sat down.

"What do we do if somebody comes?" Lewis asked.

"If they're coming up, we start down. If they're coming in here to use the stairs, we go out onto the floor. Just go opposite the way they're going. Either way, keep your head down."

"Then what?"

"Then it depends. If they get a good look, we go home. If not, we come back here and wait for Mom to go get breakfast."

"How do you know when she'll go?"

"Mom is always on some internal clock. Breakfast at nine. If she doesn't get coffee by nine-fifteen, then watch out."

"It's five after now," Lewis said, looking at his phone. "Oh, crap. Ted, did you turn your phone off?"

"Good thinking, Lew. Thanks." They waited, but not long.

* * *

"Okay, teddy bear, sleep a little. I'll read the paper and have some coffee downstairs, then I'll be back up with your big-boy breakfast," Jill said, as she closed the door and headed for the elevator.

"Let's go," Ted said. "Head down, and wait until he opens the door. Then come in, quick."

"Got it. Go."

Jack was surprised to see Ted in the hallway, but he feigned joviality. "Well, hello, Ted. What are you doing here?" He didn't acknowledge Lewis.

Ted stepped in quickly, Lewis right behind.

"What the hell?" Jack said, as Ted pulled the Smith revolver out of his pocket and said, "Back up against the window. We have to talk, and I don't have much time."

Jack complied, confused as much as frightened. "Ted, whatever you have to say to me, you don't need a gun to say it."

"I want you to listen real good, Jack. Stay away from my mother. That means all the time. That means forever. You understand?"

"I understand," Jack said, and he doubled over, gripping his chest. "I, uh… help me!"

Ted broke character and looked for a place to help Jack sit down, and the big old guy lunged at Ted, smashing him against the opposite wall. Ted broke free, aimed the gun, and… *click. Click, click, click, click, click.* "Shit," was all he had time to say.

Jack lunged again, coming at Ted with his briefcase, the only weapon in his line of sight. He pushed Ted against the wall with it, deciding his next move, when he suddenly fell to the floor. Lewis, empty champagne bottle dripping water from the ice bucket, stood over him. Jack moved, groaned, and Lewis hit him again, hard, on the back of his head. Blood came out Jack's ears. He was face down, more blood spilling onto the carpet. He wasn't breathing. Lewis looked at Ted.

Ted looked at Lewis and said, "Shit, let's get out of here!"

Lewis dropped the bottle.

Ted took Jack's wristwatch, then opened the door with his sweatshirt. *No prints*. He was thinking like he had been scripted. And they scurried down the nine flights of stairs, looking only at their feet, heads covered, and out to their bikes.

They put on their cover clothes and split up.

* * *

Back at the dorm, Ted spoke first."You asshole," he said. "You almost got me killed. No bullets? What were you thinking?"

"I was thinking, you promised under duress, and if we got in a tight spot, you'd forget all about your promise."

"You thought I'd break my promise?"

"Well?" The talk ended.

Lewis and Ted both took showers, then did laundry, part of their Sunday routine. Everything had to look routine. While the dryers were spinning, Lewis said, "Why'd you take his watch? What're you going to do with it?"

"It's gone," Ted said. "I threw it in the Olentangy."

"But why?"

"Why'd I take it? Make it look like a robbery. I couldn't think of anything else to take."

They went back to their room, started to put their clothes away. "Oh, crap," Ted said. "I didn't remember to turn my phone back on."

"Me, neither," Lewis said. When his phone lit up, he said, "Good. No messages."

Ted was pale. "I've got, like, five calls from my Mom. I gotta call her back."

"Hi, Mom," Ted said, cheerfully as he could fake it.

"Ted. Now listen to me," Jill said. "This is bad. Sit down."

"I'm sitting. What's wrong, Mom?"

"Jack is dead."

"Dead? *Dead?* What happened? Are you okay? Were you with him? Are you all right? Where are you?" *Laying it on a little thick, maybe. No, I sound shocked. She won't notice, anyway, she's so freaked out.*

"I'm at the police station." She asked where, aside. "At Substation Five, Eleventh and Cleveland. Can you get here?"

"I'm on my way, Mom. I'll be right there. Are you okay?"

"I'm okay. I'm just… hurry, please hurry."

* * *

Ted arrived at the station, out of breath. He ran to his mother, who stood up from her metal bench, sobbing. She held out her arms. He hugged her, she hugged back. "Oh, Ted," she sobbed.

After a moment, a police officer tapped Ted's shoulder and said, "Son, could we talk with you? Come with me," and he led Ted down an algae colored corridor to a room with mud-colored walls. On the table sat a pair of microphones. There was a camera in the corner opposite where he motioned Ted to sit.

"Could I ask you a few questions, Ted? On the record?" He turned on the mics and the red light on the camera lit up.

"Sure, officer. Sure. But is my mom really okay? Did he hurt her? She said he was dead. How?"

"All in good time, Ted. You mom's okay. That's all you need to think about right now. She's okay. Settle down." He pushed a bottle of water across the table. "Water?"

"Thanks."

"Now, Ted, you understand I have to ask you some questions. Your mom was the first upon a murder scene, and…"

"*Murder* scene? Jack was murdered? She said he was dead. I thought maybe a heart attack or something."

"Murdered in the hotel room. What I want to know is, when was the last time you saw Jack?"

"Uhhh… he was at our house last, uh, Spring Break. Half a year ago, a little more."

"And when did you last see your mom, I mean, before this morning?"

"Yesterday."

"Did she seem all right to you? I mean, was she nervous, uptight, anything?"

"No. She didn't like it that I bugged her about Jack. I don't, didn't, like him. He hit her. And he came on to me."

"We know about the restraining order. He came on to you? Tell me."

"It was at Christmas. He gave me an expensive watch, then later he put his hand on my thigh."

"Are you sure he was coming on to you?"

"He did it twice. The second time for sure there was no mistake."

"Does your mom know about this?"

"No, I just told her he gives me the creeps. She knows I don't like him. Didn't, I mean."

The officer changed direction. "What were you doing this morning, say, nine, ten o'clock?"

Ted thought fast. *Maybe somebody saw me. Maybe he knows already.* "I started to go for a bike ride. It was such a nice morning. But I went back. I have too much stuff to do. I washed my clothes at the dorm."

"Anybody see you?"

"On the ride, I don't know. Probably. Maybe, but I don't remember anybody I know. But laundry, yes. My roommate…"

"Lewis," the cop said. Ted nodded. "He go for a ride, too?"

"No, er, I don't know. Yes. I mean, no, he didn't go. I woke him up and we went down to do laundry together."

"When did you get back to your room? I mean, is that where you went when you finished your laundry?"

"Around ten. Yes, we went straight back up."

"Why did your mom have to call you so many times before you called her?"

"I had my phone off. It charges faster that way. I forgot to turn it back on."

"Can I see it? Do you have it with you?" Ted handed him the phone. The officer said, "Battery's half gone already."

Ted said, "It's getting soft. It was just about dead when I plugged it in. Uses a lot of power when the GPS is on, too. I had to turn that on to find the station."

"You couldn't find this place without GPS?" He was more disgusted with this millennial's total
dependence on tech than he was surprised that Ted couldn't find a station that was less than a mile from campus on well-known streets.

"Never been here before."

The officer handed the phone back to Ted, who took it with a noticeably shaking hand. "Thank you, Ted. Now, let's go see your mother."

* * *

Jill was in another room with another officer when Ted got to the lobby.

The officer said, "She'll be out pretty soon. Want some more water? Coke or something? Granola bar?"

"Granola bar would be great, thanks. I haven't had breakfast yet."

"You'll be out of here soon, son," he said, as he handed Ted the bar and another pint of water.

When he was alone, Ted texted Lewis. *You were sleeping before we did laundry.* He sent it, then cleared the message.

Jill and another officer came out. Ted stood up and went to hug his mom. "You two can talk all you want, now," the officer said. You're free to go. Please, though, don't say anything to anybody about this. Especially the press, okay?"

"What should I say?" Jill said. "I mean, it'll be all over the place."

"Just tell them it's under investigation, and you've been asked to not talk to anybody, and to please leave you alone."

"Okay, we can do that. Thank you, officer. Now, what should I do?"

"Anything you want. Why not go to brunch with your son? They'll be processing your room for another hour or so. We'll call you when you can go back, pick up your things."

"Thanks again, officer." And she started sobbing again, leaning on Ted as they left the station.

* * *

"Mom, I'll drive," Ted said. As soon as I take my bike apart. It'll fit in the trunk if I take the wheels off." He looked in the trunk. "Is it okay if I use these newspapers to protect the carpet?"

"Sure," Jill said. "They're just going to recycling, anyway."

As they headed to breakfast, Ted said, "Can I call Lewis? He must be wondering what happened." She nodded, and Ted pulled out his phone and dialed. "Hi, Lew," he said. "Did you get my message?" Ted looked at his mom and whispered, "I told him you're okay."

Lewis said, "I can't talk right now, Ted. I'm talking to the police about where I was this morning. Told them about how I did laundry with you."

Ted sighed, took another breath. "Okay, Lew. Mom and I are going to brunch. Call me later, when you can."

"Sure thing, bro."

At brunch, Jill told Ted how she had gone down to the lobby to pick up breakfast for herself and Jack, and found Jack when she opened the door. "I wasn't gone twenty minutes," she said. There he was, all just lying there. Blood all over his head."

"You don't think he could have just, you know, fallen or something?"

"No, the police said it didn't look like an accident. First they thought I did it."

"*You?*"

"Well, there's the bloody champagne bottle, what they hit him with…"

"They?"

"I don't know. 'They,' 'he,' 'she,' 'it,' whoever hit him. They were looking for fingerprints, stuff that's missing, that kind of thing."

"So you just opened the door and there he is, lying on the floor? Did you know he was…?"

"Dead? I thought so right away. He wasn't moving, and there was so much blood. I didn't want him to be, but I knew. Then I called the desk – dialed 'O' for operator. I don't know why I didn't call 911. Well, yes, I didn't know how to get an outside line, forgot I had a cell phone." She let a wry smile cross her face for a second. "So they said they'd call the police, and they sent a security guy up right away. He took me out of the room, stepped over the breakfast that was on the floor by the door. I don't even remember dropping it."

"Oh, Mom," Ted said. "I'm so sorry. I was hungry. I didn't even think to see if you felt like eating. I'm so selfish."

"Don't worry about it, Ted. Everybody's got to eat. I'm hungry, too, if that helps any."

* * *

It was nearly two o'clock when Jill dropped Ted off at the dorm, Two-thirty by the time he put his bike back together and got into his room. "Lewis," he said, waking him up. Lewis, you okay?"

"Yeah," he said. "The police came here, asked me all sorts of 'Where were you?' questions. I told them I was sleeping until you woke me up to do laundry. Hope that was okay."

"That was perfect. So, you got my message."

"Message?"

"Shit, Lew, you didn't get my text? You didn't let them look at your phone, did you?"

"Well, yes, actually. I…"

"Let me see it, Lew. Let me see your phone."

Lewis hit the password and handed it to Ted. Ted looked a minute, said, "You don't have any messages from me this morning."

"No. I deleted it as soon as I saw it. How do you think I knew I was sleeping?" With a twinkle in his eye.

"Lewis, you asshole. That was not funny."

"Yes it was. But not as good as giving you an empty gun."

"That was serious. I mean, what if…"

Lewis was enjoying torturing his roommate. "What if it didn't go off? I have your back. You're covered. But what if it *did* go off? Then you've got all kinds of noise. We never get out of there. What if you miss, maybe the bullet goes through the wall, hits some poor slob next door? There's some 'what ifs' for you."

"Lewis, I promised."

"But hey, I didn't. And if you'd kept your promise you never would've found out it was empty, anyway… Forget it. You know, there's something else I never paid attention to. You know that's a five-shot gun, right?"

"Yeah. So?"

"So, there was only one live round in it. The other four were already shot."

"So it only would have gone off once? What if I missed?"

"Yeah, another what if. So, you want to go to Scott?"

"Dinner, already? Scott Hall's okay."

"It's open, and I don't know about you, but I haven't eaten yet today. How about it?"

* * *

Ted was walking fast. Lewis was surprised, working to keep up. "How's your mom?"

"How do you think?" She's confused, freaked out. Sad."

"What does she think happened?"

"So far, they think it's a robbery gone bad. They asked her about if he had a watch. She said he always had on an expensive one."

"Glad it's in the river," Lewis said. "Something I didn't tell you about the gun."

"Yeah, thanks on that. Unloaded. Big lot of good it'd have done me."

"Well, since you promised, I figured it didn't matter. Anyway, about the gun…"

"What about it?"

"When I unloaded it, that was the first time I had it open. There was only one bullet in there."

"You said, back that time it fell out of your mattress, you said it was loaded."

"I didn't even know how to check it. I don't know anything about guns."

Ted stopped walking, right there in the middle of the sidewalk, and looked at his roommate, the guy who had just probably saved his life, his partner in the crime of his life. The only crime of his straight-arrow, boring, young life. "Lewis, do you think?" And he stopped.

"I looked at the last one, the one that hadn't been shot." Lewis looked at Ted to be sure he was listening. He was. "Ted, it didn't match any of the ammo you and I researched. I couldn't find a single thirty-eight Special looked like that, in any of the ammo catalogs on line. I think my dad made it."

"Where is all his reloading stuff?"

"Sherry sold it after, to a guy. She sold all his stuff after he died."

They started walking again. "So, you have that last bullet?"

"Yeah." Then Lewis said, "Do you think we should give it to Leonard?"

Ted thought for a minute. "No. Let's take it apart and weigh the slug, see if it matches. See how to do it on YouTube. See if it's one-fifteen…"

"God, Ted. I don't like thinking about this."

"Right now Lewis, we should be thinking about this morning, what we're going to say, do. Did you get rid of the outside stuff? Your shoes?"

"Forgot about the shoes. I'm wearing them right now. I like these. They're comfy."

"Yeah, well, get rid of them. Put them in the Goodwill box. And get another pair, like, at Goodwill, shoes that are all broken in, fit okay, but different. Six bucks. Can't beat Goodwill. Damn it, I had to get rid of my rain suit."

"You never wore it anyway."

"Put it in a dumpster near the hotel. Some homeless guy's going to like it. It'll be gone before the police even start checking stuff, in case they saw me in it in the first place."

They arrived at Scott, got dinner, sat down and went over the timeline, getting their stories straight. "It's simple, really," Ted said. "Everything's just what happened until this morning. I woke you up and we did laundry, like we usually do on Sundays. I left my phone in the room."

"I thought you had it turned off," Lewis reminded him.

"Yeah, turned off. It charges faster that way. In the room. Then I called Mom, and everything after that was the same, too."

"As long as they don't get us on video," Lewis said.

"Or if somebody recognizes us on our bikes, coming or going. Did you see anybody you knew? I didn't. I'm pretty sure."

"Me, neither. And I kept my head down riding the bike. Shit."

"What?"

"I looked up at a couple of street signs on the way to the hotel. If they had cameras there…"

"I think I did, too, but we were in different places, different times. All we can do is hope they didn't see us. Then our stories go away." Ted looked sick.

Lewis said, "Best thing to do, not say another thing. Don't help. They'll never catch us without we screw it up, talking."

"Doesn't that make us more of suspects?"

"Ted, we're already suspects. But we don't have much of a motive, none they can prove, and nobody can place us anywhere. They got nothing. Let's not give them something. Did you leave any fingerprints? You did all the doorknobs with your sweatshirt, right?"

"Yeah, good on that. You touch the bottle anywhere?"

"Sure. I had to pick it up. But I grabbed it on the foil, up by the neck. The rest of it was dripping wet, anyway."

"No blood on either of us, right? You didn't step in any?"

Lewis said, "The way I saw it, he didn't start to bleed until he was on the floor. No, I didn't step in anything. And I'm getting rid of these shoes, and yours are gone. And the watch is gone. The only thing could mess it up is somebody saw us, recognized us, or…"

"Or what?" Ted tensed up.

"Or came to our room while we were gone, and the cops ask them."

"Long shot," Ted said. "First, that anybody's up and looking for us on a Sunday morning, and second, that they'd find just that person and ask them the right question, and get the time right, too. We're not there, maybe doing laundry, maybe their recollection of time is off a few minutes."

"Let's hope," Lewis said, and they were back in their room, studying, just like everybody else in the dorm.

Chapter Twenty-one: We have to talk

The matron handed Jill all her things in the hotel lobby. "If you think something's missing, call me," the matron said. "We kept a few things as evidence, but most everything that we think might be yours is in the box. Here's my card and the case number."

"Thank you, uhhh," she looked at the card, "Officer Martin. You have my number, address, and all that, in case you need it?"

"Yes, Missus Hamlin. Are you okay to drive home? Do you need to stay in town another day? Is there anything I can do for you?"

"I'll be okay. I've just got to get home, lie down, that's all."

"Safe trip."

"Thanks." And Jill put her things from the box into her rollerboard, listened to the wheels clack-clack down the hall and out the door. She tossed it into the back seat of the Taurus, got in, sat down, put the key in the ignition… and burst into silent tears.

How long she was there, she didn't keep track. But the sun was low in the sky when she sat up straight, wiped her eyes, and determinately headed out of the parking lot toward Mansfield.

She reached for her phone to call Jack, but realized he would never answer. She dialed anyway, to hear his voice one more time. She left a message. "Jack, I know you can't hear me.

I just wanted to say 'good-bye, I love you,' one more time. Good-bye, Jack." She hung up, feeling better and worse at the same time.

* * *

"Sherry, yeah, it's me. Are you okay? I have something to tell you. Important. Ted's mother's boyfriend, Jack, he's…"

"He's dead, isn't he?" Sherry said. "The TV said some lawyer from Dayton was murdered in a fancy hotel in Columbus this morning. No suspects, no details until next of kin are notified."

"That's him, Sherry. News travels fast. Ted's mom is pretty broken up about it. She told Ted she went down to get breakfast, came back up, and there he was, dead on the floor."

"Do you know what happened?"

"No, not really. She's already headed back home. She took Ted to brunch, lunch, whatever – but they didn't talk much about it, from what he told me. I haven't seen her since you were there with us."

"Poor Jill," Sherry said. "She was counting on something developing with Jack, wasn't she?"

"I don't know, Sherry, really. It wasn't all roses, according to Ted. But yeah, he was her boyfriend. That has to mean something, right?"

"I imagine it has to. I don't know. I haven't dated since your dad…"

"Oh, sorry, sorry. I'm just not thinking about anything right now except poor Miss Jill."

"What about Ted?"

"Well, Ted's sorry for his mom, but he never liked Jack, from what he says. So, he's sad for his mom. And even if he didn't like Jack, I don't think he'd prefer him dead."

"I know, Lewis. There's a lot of people we can do without, but it's God's choice, not ours."

"Amen to that. Say, have you heard anything else from that officer, Leonard?"

"About your father? No. Why would I?"

"I just thought that, you know, with the extra evidence…"

"Seems the case is as cold as ever. What do you plan to do, supposing you solve it somehow?"

"I don't know. Just closure, I guess. I shouldn't say this, but I was talking with Ted about it. The whole murder, how he treated you, how he treated me. I told Ted I'd like to solve the case just so I could shake the guy's hand. But I know that's not a nice thing to say."

"Lewis, that's a terrible thing to say! He was your father."

"He was a drunk. He was abusive. He hit you, more than once, and he was… bad to you."

"I know. You're right. But I hate hearing a son talk like that about his father, no matter how bad the relationship was."

"Well, it was. And it's not like I go around telling people this. It was just to Ted."

"Some advice, Lewis? Keep that kind of thought under your hat. Don't share it, even with your best friend."

"Even with you?"

"Too late for that, isn't it? But seriously, you never know when that kind of talk will hit somebody just a little the wrong way, and it will boomerang, I promise you."

"I know. I know, Sherry. It's just… it's so close to me. I mean, Ted's my best friend, and Miss Jill, she's…"

"You have feelings for her?"

"Uh – What? No, not like that. I mean, she was so sad, Ted said. And Ted's a mess about it."

"You had me worried for a minute. I know she's beautiful. I saw her myself. But she's, well, I don't have to say it. You know."

"I have to admit, yeah, I've noticed she's beautiful. I can't help noticing. But yeah, me, too. I know what you mean. Don't worry."

Sherry changed tone. "When will you be able to visit here?"

"Thanksgiving's coming up. I'll come home instead of to Ted's, like last year. Is that soon enough?"

"That will have to do, Lewis. Now, I know you have a lot more to do than think about that awful stuff. Try to keep your head on straight. Study. And I'll see you in a couple weeks. I love you."

"Love you, Sherry. And thanks."

* * *

Ted's phone buzzed. "Hi, Jessica. What's up?"

"We have to talk."

Ted laughed. "That's never good, what you said. I'll come over at seven?"

"The phone's okay for this. Ted?"

"Yes?"

"You've been weird, really weird, lately."

"Sorry. Yeah, I know. My mom's boyfriend, he… Well, you know."

"Ever since then. Look, Ted, you're a great lab partner."

"Jess?"

"That's all I want to be, from now on. If that's not okay, you'll need a new lab partner."

"Jessica? Jess?" Can we talk about this?" Ted was talking on a dead line.

Ted ran to Jessica's dorm, waited for a girl to come out, and ran in, up the stairs, turned right, to her room. She was waiting for him, door open.

"Hi, Ted," she said calmly, even as Ted was sweating and wheezing. "Sit down."

There was nowhere to sit but the floor. There was junk on Jessica's roommate's chair, and she made no motion to move it. Jessica sat on the other chair. Ted sat on the floor, cross-legged, heart pounding, having no clue where to start. But he started. "Jess, I thought we had something. I... I might even love you."

"Ted, I really like you. Well, until Halloween, anyway. I was thinking about breaking up with you before that, anyway. My dad..."

"What? Your dad told you to break up with me?"

"No, that was my idea. He wanted me to keep going out with you."

"Why? I never met him. What did you tell him?"

"Nothing. It just seems that, well, he met your mom, and, well, he, I don't know -- I think he wants us to be together so he can keep seeing your mom. It's just... crazy."

"Yeah, it's crazy, all right. So why are you dumping me? You said I'm a good lab partner. That's something, isn't it?"

"Ted, I don't w want to lose you as a lab partner, just as a boyfriend. Besides, I'm leaving at the end of the year. I got a big scholarship at University of Dayton, going to live at home. Dad's getting divorced. He's going to need me."

"So, we're...?"

"I'll see you in lab, Ted. It's been nice."

Chapter Twenty-two: Jill turns a page

Jill had rearranged the house so Ted barely recognized it. The furniture was the same, but every room save the guest bedroom and kitchen had everything in a new place.

The pictures on the walls, in their spots since forever, were in different places, different rooms. The carpets – there were places badly worn, but now cleaned and under furniture rather than alongside it. Some area rugs gave a new feel.

And "What's that? One wall's blue, used to match," Ted said.

"That's an 'accent wall.' They say it makes rooms look bigger. I think it looks like I ran out of paint," Jill said. "But I kind of like that deep blue with the rest of the room in that cream color."

"Makes the old color look like it's a hundred years old," Ted said. "I liked it the old way. But looking at this, maybe make all the walls that – what color is that?"

"That's called Colonial Blue."

"Make them all that Colonial Blue, and use the old color for trim. Maybe that would look good. But hey, I hardly live here any more. It's up to you." He looked at his mom, so little-looking, not the confident ball-buster he was used to seeing, always in charge. Not the 'hot mama' people saw when they went anywhere together. More like a *girl*, but an old girl, sad and alone and scared. And vulnerable.

She took his laid her head on his shoulder and cried a little. "All my men gone, all at once," she said. I've got to make some changes. I'm thirty-eight, you know. Doors are closing fast. I don't have a career. I mean, the Tourist Center is fine part-time work, and I like people, and I know a lot about Mansfield, and all that, but, really, I've always relied on a man."

"Mom, Jack was bad news. He wasn't worthy of you."

"You don't know the half of it, Ted. Did you know he was married?"

"Married? Hell, no, I… I mean, no, Mom, I didn't. You always told me he was divorced. When did you find out? How did he? I mean, he always seemed to have time on holidays and all."

"He was *getting* a divorce. They lived apart. But yes, he was married."

"Mom, I know you liked him, but I could never stand him. He was a slime-ball." He looked at his mom, her eyes cast to the floor. "I mean, Mom, you had no way of knowing…"

She accepted Ted's back-pedal. "But he had good parts, too, Ted. And I don't know what to do on my own. I've never been on my own, for any time at all. I was with my parents until I eloped with your father. Then, there was Bill. He was too old, but he was good. You don't remember him, do you?"

"Mom, he died when I was five. I was four when you met. No, I don't remember Bill. I've only seen two pictures of him in my life."

"Well, Bill and I were going to get married. He was 'too old.' I laugh now. He was forty. Of course, I was what, twenty-three when he died? Twenty-two, with a toddler." She looked up at the ceiling and sighed. "Anyway, he and I were going to get married. He lived right here."

"I remember that," Ted said.

"He lived here, and he took out life insurance for us. That took care of the house. It's ours. But I still had to work, put food on the table, pay taxes, insurance, get money together for your college…"

"You've always worked, Mom. I know that. And I wish I could contribute while I'm in school, but…"

"It's not about you, Ted. You're the child. I'm the mom." She looked him in the eyes. "I know it's my responsibility to be the mom, and you've always been a good son. Don't worry; your student loans are manageable, and," she winked, "they're yours as soon as you can take them on. But we're good, for now. And forever. You just worry about school, about getting a job after, about your own family. Mom can take care of herself."

"You won't have to," Ted said. "I'll make sure you're always okay, one way or another. A couple years, and I'll be making good money, enough for both of us."

She looked at him in a strange way, as if she were talking to a five-year-old. A hundred and fifty pound, five-ten, five year old college sophomore who shaved. "Ted, you're so deep in school right now, you aren't looking ahead. In a very short time, you're going to be on a career path, probably starting your own family."

She put her hands on his shoulders. "You aren't going to be living here forever. You're going to leave, have your own children, your own wife, your own bills, your own problems. In a couple years, that won't be 'your room' any more. This probably won't even be 'your house.' Or mine, for that matter. Ted, we're going in different directions, and in a very short time. Three more Christmases here. Four, maybe, if you bring your wife to celebrate with me. Five, and I'll be a grandmother." She could see he was crumbling. "Okay, six or seven, maybe. No sense rushing grandmotherhood." They both smiled.

She held him. They made no sound, but both were sobbing.

Chapter Twenty-three:
Getting to know Mom

Rain was turning to the first snow of the season in Chillicothe. Lewis helped Sherry set the table for two. "Sherry, I'm so happy you're doing the roast for Thanksgiving. I mean, I love turkey, but your roast is soooo good."

"Thanks, Lewis. Happy Thanksgiving. I'm so glad you're here with me. Just us, but it's so nice to relax here, be with you. I mean, I like Ted. I like his mom, too. But Thanksgiving is really a family thing, and, well, we're a good little family."

"We are. I really appreciate you, Sherry. You are such a good woman, and such a good mom to me."

"Mom?" She looked straight into his eyes. "You never called me Mom."

"I thought you didn't want me to," he said.

"Once. I don't know what I was thinking. I remember the time. Maybe I was playing hard to get. I don't know. But I always thought you would try again."

"I was so shocked, and," he looked down, "I was so hurt. I never wanted to try again. Or, really... I never wanted to be rejected like that again. I never got over it."

"Lewis, I'm so sorry. I never meant it to be a permanent thing, and I certainly didn't mean to hurt you. So, so sorry." She cried a little. They finished dinner in silence.

"Can we talk in the living room? I'd like to talk about some other serious stuff."

"About school?"

"About Dad."

* * *

He sat on the big chair, Sherry on the sofa, so close their knees almost touched. She said, "Can I go first?"

Lewis looked confused. "Uh, sure. But what's on my mind is important."

"Lewis, this is the most important thing I've ever said to you. You need to pay attention."

"I'm paying attention," he said, squirming. "So, what's so important?"

"Lewis, I saw you and Ted at the hotel that Sunday morning."

"What?"

"That Sunday morning when Jack was killed." Lewis leaned forward. "What? I mean, that's impossible. I was sleeping, and you – you were home. You left Saturday."

"No, you weren't. And no, I didn't." She looked straight in his eyes. "I was there."

"But how?"

"Jill and I talked while you and Ted were out getting drinks, or maybe when you were scoping out the hotel. We hit it off great. She's an interesting lady. You'd never guess what she told me."

He swallowed. "I probably wouldn't. What did she tell you?"

"More like, asked me." Sherry got up, walked into the kitchen while Lewis stewed on the couch. "You want a Pepsi?" she asked.

"Uhhh, yeah. Thanks."

Sherry returned with vodka on the rocks and a can of diet. "Oh," she began, handing Lewis the cold can and taking her time getting settled back onto the sofa, "she asked me if you and Ted were, you know, gay. For each other."

Lewis was so relieved, and so surprised, he just started laughing. "Gay? That's just crazy. How could she think like that?"

"It's just that, well, Ted doesn't talk about anybody at school except you. I told her that you don't talk about anybody but Ted… and her."

Lewis decided silence was his only friend. Sherry continued.

"So I told her that I was certain you weren't, and if you weren't, then he couldn't be, at least for you. Then she said something strange."

"What'd she say?"

"She said she should have realized you weren't gay."

"Me? But Ted might be? But…"

"Like I said, strange. I let it go. But now, you can tell me what she meant."

Lewis just looked at her.

"It can't be as bad as what happened up in that hotel room. It's truth time, Lewis."

"So that's how you were there? Miss Jill thinks we're gay? Where did you stay? We only paid for one night."

"She wanted to see me, and Sunday breakfast was her only chance. So she paid for the hotel, one more night. But you're evading the question. How did she figure you weren't gay, but she wasn't sure of her own son?"

"You know about Nicole."

"This wasn't about Nicole."

"Did she tell you?"

"Didn't have to. I could tell, myself. Every time you mentioned Ted's mom, you had a bulge in your pants. She said she noticed, too."

"The Mystery of The Telltale Dong?"

"Moms notice. No mystery."

Lewis started laughing. He was trying to think, fast, about why that was so funny. "So you think I think she's uh, what? Hot?"

"Don't you? If you don't, there's at least a part of you that isn't convinced. Oh, come on. I know. Admit it."

"Yeah, she's probably the only older woman I ever looked at more than once in my life. She's just so… so, so beautiful. She's perfect."

"She's also your best friend's mom. You start showing, you can't keep it a secret. Just go take a cold shower, or think of brussels sprouts."

"Brussels sprouts? What'll that do?"

"You'll think of something else. And before Ted catches on, I'd advise that you be aware of the signals you're sending. You look foolish, and Ted won't appreciate it."

"You said she noticed?"

"Yes, she noticed. She got a kick out of it. Thinks it's cute."

Sherry got up to get another vodka rocks. When she repositioned herself on the couch, she said, "Your turn. What's so important?"

Lewis wanted to focus, but he kept thinking. *Cute?*

"Okay, well. It's about Dad. Ted and I think we know what happened."

"Please," Sherry said. She settled back in the couch.

"Here's what we think. First, no witnesses except you."

"I was right here, waiting for your dad, and I heard the shots."

"Okay; I'm just laying this out. Next, they spent maybe no time at all looking for evidence. We found the shells in the matter of a couple hours, three years after. They couldn't have missed five shells."

"You found four," she corrected.

"And they found one more, after our four. Then, there's the question of why the shells don't match up. Four nine millimeter, two three-eighties. None of them match, either each other or even calibers. Those shells weren't fired at the scene, or by the same gun. They were planted."

"So, who would have planted them? And why?"

"The killer. Why? To throw off the investigation. But there's more here, in the shells."

Sherry drained her glass, crunched an ice cube. "There's more. There's six shells, four shots, two three-eighties. Whoever tossed those shells didn't know the difference between a three-eighty and a nine millimeter."

"Why do you think they tossed shells? Doesn't the gun just spit them out? And the bullets – they couldn't compare them enough to know if they came from the same gun, but they were the same type and weight – and they were from a nine millimeter." Sherry had been paying attention.

"A revolver doesn't throw shells," Lewis said.

"But a revolver doesn't use those bullets, either, right? Doesn't a revolver use bigger bullets? That's what you told me, right?"

"But a guy who reloads his ammo can load any bullet he wants, and Dad had a reloading setup. He could load bullets for a nine into a thirty-eight. He could make it look like a nine did the shooting, never leave a shell casing behind."

"But he wouldn't shoot himself, even if he did. And not four times." Sherry hadn't connected the dots.

"No, but it would make the gun untraceable. Whoever looked for the gun, would be looking for a nine, not a thirty-eight. And shells don't always match each other, even if they're fired from the same gun, so he could use random shells, if he wanted the match to look convincing."

Sherry was leaning back in the sofa, the two vodkas fully absorbed. "Where are you going with this?"

"Here's what we think happened: Dad came home and somebody was waiting for him, caught him just as he approached the front stoop. Shot him four times with a thirty-eight revolver loaded with nine-millimeter slugs. The killer probably already tossed some shells into the bushes."

"But there were six shells, and two didn't even match," Sherry said.

"Right. The killer didn't know the difference, and thought the revolver was a six-shooter, and planned to usc all six. So the killer planted the six shells ahead of time, maybe not wanting the smell of them to linger, or not to be in his pocket or laundry."

"What are you saying? The killer knew someone would be looking for nine-millimeter shells?"

"Exactly. But it only took four shots, and the killer forgot about the shells, hid the gun. It was never identified, was it?"

"No. They never found it."

"And that's because it was in our attic, where I found it a year ago, and I've had it ever since."

"You took a gun to school?" Sherry was shocked, angry, confused.

"You know what I did over Halloween weekend. I know what you did to Dad."

She stared.

"Look, You thought it was a six-shooter. Most revolvers are. Most thirty-eights are. You shot four times, and you hid the gun. There was still one round in it. I took it apart. The bullet was for a nine, loaded in a thirty-eight case. Dad reloaded for lots of the guys. He was cheap, probably used their bullets in his own reloads. They're fine for practice, and he got 'em free, so he used them. That's what I think."

"And?"

"And he finally abused us once too often, and you shot him. The rest of the police couldn't stand him. They knew what he did to you, maybe even to me. He didn't make any friends at the prison. Nobody liked him. So they did a little investigation, found nothing, and shoved it aside as soon as other crimes came across their desks.

"You were the only witness. They didn't look hard for another. They knew you wouldn't cause any more trouble; you're not a killer. This was self-defense, defense of me, too. So the case went away. The only reason anything else happened was that Ted and I got our noses into it."

"What did you think, as you went along, you and Ted playing detectives?"

"First, I thought it was that detective, Clayton Yarbrough. Went to Arizona right after. But I checked up on him, too. He was Mister Rules & Regulations. Not the guy to use homemade ammo."

"So when did you figure it out?"

"Ted did, mostly. We were trying to think of why a cop would toss three-eighty shells when he was trying to make it like a nine did it. A cop wouldn't. A cop would know how many shots were in his own revolver, too. So Ted figured it had to be somebody who was close to that weapon, but who didn't know much about it. And I found the gun in the attic, and only four chambers had been fired, and the fifth bullet – the one still in the gun -- matched the bullet in Dad, and in the ground. It was you. Couldn't be anybody else."

She looked at him, stood up. So did he. She said, "What do you plan to do now?"

"We're family. Here's your gun back, Mom. I love you."

"Just one more mystery, Lewis. Can I ask?"

"Sure, Mom." It felt good, it felt right to call her 'Mom.'

"Remember when that officer needed your phone, and you wrote your password in his little book?" Lewis nodded. "And then he dropped it, and I picked it up and gave it back to him?"

"Sort of. Yeah, I..."

"Why was your password, 'Jill69?'"

- ooo -

Epilogue

Most epilogues wrap up the story in a plausible way, a way that allows justice to triumph. Good guys get rewards; bad guys get punished.

But here's what happened in our story:

Nicole went to Hollywood to act, but soon became homeless. A producer saw her on television in a soup line at Thanksgiving, tracked her down, and offered her a part as a famous but fading actress's drug-addicted daughter. She took the part and began a new career.

Jessica Zitkowski graduated with a degree in Chemistry and moved to China to formulate knock-off pharmaceuticals. Her father, Charles, was strangled in his office by a jealous husband.

Ted moved back home with Jill after he graduated with honors. He never married; he worked as a pharmacist's assistant in the local Walmart Super Center for the next fifteen years. Jill stayed on with the tourism job, until arthritis kept her home. When Jill died, he sold the house, emptied his bank account, bought a Harley, and headed west. The bike was declared abandoned after six months in a parking lot near LAX. There was speculation that he had flown to China to look for Jessica.

***

Lewis called Sherry 'Mom' until she passed away from pneumonia two years after this book first went to press, three days after he graduated.

At her wake, Officer Leonard shook Lewis's hand.

"When did you know?" he asked the grieving son.

"Know what?" was the predictable reply. They walked off to a private spot. Lewis looked into the officer's inquisitive but firm eyes. Lewis said, "Maybe I could ask you when *you* knew."

Leonard put his arm around young Lewis's shoulder. "We knew all along. You know, you and your friend, you almost blew it all up."

Lewis lurched back, then assumed a casual look.

"If you knew, why didn't you…?"

"For the same reason you never told us." Leonard saw that Lewis was crying. "So, you want to give us the gun? We can run ballistics, close the case."

Lewis thought a moment. "No. I think I just want the case out there. It doesn't matter any more, and I don't want all these people who loved my mom to think of what she did, even if it was the right thing."

The murder case of Garret Foreman again went cold, with a few more pieces of evidence in the box. And Patrolman Leonard continued to keep the case of the murdered lawyer in his near-conscious. *Maybe some day...*

#

About Tim Kern

The author is best known as an aviation writer, with bylined features in over fifty aviation publications worldwide. Unlike his usual fare, however, this book contains no verifiable facts, and the people and their quotes are all made up.

Kern taught economics for fifteen years, to students from high school through postgraduate levels.

His nine-year radio show, *Tim Kern, Talking Sense*, aired on over 200 stations. He raced motorcycles and still rides regularly; he's a former car racer and race instructor, and he was a professional mechanic on a championship-winning Can-Am team.

He holds a Private Pilot certificate.

He has other published titles, including his first book, <u>The Executive Primer</u> (serialized over three years in *SUCCESS Magazine*). His crime novels, published as part of the Mystery One™ Series, represent a new venture.

Other Book Titles by Tim Kern

Non-fiction, how-to:
The Executive Primer
The Manual by Eduardo
The Americans' Fight to Survive (co-author, credited as editor)

Fiction:
EGOFALL: Ego. Paranoia. Murder
Caught by a Cat: Not a childrens' book

To receive advance notice of new books and occasional free short stories by Tim Kern, send an email with "FUTURE WORKS" as the subject to
INFO@TIMKERN.COM

Connect with Tim Kern

If you enjoyed this book, please take the time to write a review, and by all means, tell others (and naturally if you didn't, don't). There are a few ways to stay in touch with the author.

His Facebook page, Writings of Tim Kern, is one such method.
[https://www.facebook.com/TimKernWritings/]
Direct email is another. See below.

Tim is available for speaking engagements and book signings.

At the risk of sounding redundant, to get on Tim Kern's email list (and receive periodic free short stories and articles, questions, and advance notice of upcoming publications), send an email request to INFO@TIMKERN.COM

**Please remember to leave a review
of my book at your favorite retailer.**

THANK YOU.